DANK HOUSE MANOR PUBLISHING

Dedication

For my family who have stuck with me through thick and thin. Thank you for all your support over the last several years.

Thoughts from a Barbed Wire Fence

A Collection of Short Stories and a Novella

By

J.E. Badham

CONTENTS

Free-lancing

"Tom? Tom Bristal?"

"Mark. What the hell you doin' these days?"

"Insurance. Interested?"

"No thanks. The wife and kids are well looked after."

"Wife? Kids? You?"

"Believe it or not. What about you? Ever get married?"

"Yeah, but it didn't work out. So, did you bring her with you?"

"Sure. I married Pam. You know, Pam Martin."

"You're kidding?"

"No. We've got three kids. Two boys and a girl."

"Jeez, things change. I'd never have figured you for the family type."

"Look, there's Rob."

"Tom. I was just talking to Pam. Quite the happy home-maker. Hi Mark. I hear you got yourself into insurance. Things sure have changed since high school, eh? Did you hear Melissa and Dave Allen got married? And Richard, he made it through med-school--Dr. Phillips, ooh. Seems so weird. Oh jeez, there's Jeff. Gotta go. I'll talk to you guys later. Take care, eh."

"Well there's one guy who hasn't changed."

"Everybody's friend and nobody's friend."

"Want another beer?"

"No thanks, I'm driving."

"Okay. I'll see ya later. Say hi to Pam for me."

"Yeah. Take it easy."

"Hi Tom."

"Lisa!"

"You remembered."

"How could I forget?"

"Some do."

"Not me. What're you doin' now?"

"Free-lancing for the 'Star'."

"Yeah? What kind of stories?"

"Whatever catches my eye. I do a lot of--oh shit. I'm sorry."

"No. No. Don't worry about it, it's an old jacket. You okay?"

"Yeah. Just a few too many. I'm really sorry."

"It's nothing. Don't worry."

"I'd better go; it's a little noisy in here."

"Sure. It was great to see you again."

"You too. Bye."

"Honey."

"Pam. Careful. Jeez, you and Lisa would make a good pair."

"Lisa?"

"Forget it. You wanna get some air?"

"Gweat. Oops."

"Here, let me hold your drink."

"Promise you won't drink any?"

"I promise. Let's go."

"My jacket."

"Believe me, you won't need it."

"Did you see Dan? He's got his own business."

"Really? No, I didn't see him."

"You didn't walk around--oh, that feels good."

"It's a nice night."

"Don't walk too far. Can we sit?"

"Sure. Here, sit on my jacket."

"Thanks Hun. You put up with a lot."

"It's your night."

"It's always my night. Don't shwug your shoulders. It's true."

"It's okay."

"Tom. Pam. I'm glad I found you guys. Rob's made his final statement."

"His what?"

"He hung himself in the bathroom. A note attached to his chest that said something about not being able to keep up--ever. No. Don't bother going in. He's a mess. They're clearing the place out. The reunion's over."

"Can I do anything?"

"Just keep the ladies calm. Looks like Pam's gonna pass out."

"Honey?"

"Why would he do it?"

"I don't know. I don't know."

"Maybe he saw the world for what it was."

"Lisa? Lisa! Where're you going?"

"Got a story to write. I need details."

Mary-Anne

Two years ago something happened to me that changed my whole life. And now, just because the damn janitor found me before I could lose enough blood, the mind-rapers want to hear about it. But they don't want to listen to anything; they just want to change it. So, I thought I'd write it all down, so they can't, change it. I also thought that maybe there's someone out there who understands; although, from my previous experiences with your world and its inhabitants, I doubt it. The mind-invaders call it "psychosis"; but I don't believe that. I believe it's real; it's far from crazy to me. I prefer to call it a "lucid ego aperture", if they want to get psychological about it.

I told you it happened two years ago, well the exact date was January 15th, 2014--a Wednesday. I was sitting in the back pew of a church, paying more attention to the hail that was stinging the stained-glass windows than to the nose-blowing and sobbing that was going on around me. Actually, I felt sick to my stomach. The mourners were making me nauseous; that's why I was listening to the hail. Unfortunately, the sound of the pellets rebounding back to nature wasn't enough to stifle the human sniffles. Fortunately, my stomach stayed intact.

So, I was sitting there alone. To the characters around me, I was an outsider; but, then again, so was the corpse. I'd never been to a funeral before; but then, neither had the corpse. We had something in common, after all. That was what I'd been looking for in her eyes, in her actions, in her feelings--something that linked me uniquely to her.

And on the day of her funeral, we were finally the same. Neither of us belonged. We were both dead among the living. But for the first time in the fifteen years of my life, it felt good--not belonging, that is.

I'd wanted to know everything about her. I felt she had something to teach me and I was starving for her knowledge. I can't explain the feeling, exactly; it's something you have to experience yourself--then again, everything is. At school, I'd take the long way to my classes and risk being late, just to catch a glimpse of her in the hallway. She was three grades ahead of me; I had her schedule memorized.

I followed her home every night, even though I lived half an hour away from the school in the opposite direction.

Most days she walked with a bunch of friends; but on Tuesdays and Thursdays she left school late--she had band practice on those nights--and walked home alone.

I read in the library during that time; and when I saw bodies passing by the window in the library door, I'd pack up my stuff and casually follow her out. I guess I wasn't casual enough though, because on Tuesday, October 7th, she stopped ahead of me and turned around. She stood, blocking the middle of the sidewalk, and stared at me. My cheeks went all hot and my heart started to race. And then she smiled, but instead of making things better, they got worse. I tripped over a crack in the crummy sidewalk and fell, kissing the pavement and tearing the skin from my palms. I couldn't move; I just lay there--frozen.

"Hey...you okay?" There was a sensitive tone to her voice as she tried to cover up the laugh.

For a second I hated her. But only for a second because in the next section I was concentrating on defending myself against the onslaught of tears that were charging up my throat; it was no use trying though, and finally I surrendered to them.

Was I disgusted with myself? You bet. But what could I do? I wasn't crying because I was hurt--I'd skinned my hands before. I was crying because I was so damn embarrassed. I shouldn't have been--I know that now--but when you're only fifteen years old and the person you're living for finally notices you...well, you'd be embarrassed too.

Anyway, I guess she didn't see me as much of a 'suck' because she let me walk home with her every Tuesday and Thursday night. On Mondays, Wednesdays, and Fridays, I'd walk behind her and her friends. I never said anything to her when there was anyone else around and she never said anything to me. It was like a secret friendship. It was more than I'd ever hoped for; but, then again, I'd never hoped for much.

"Hope" was a word I'd dropped from my vocabulary before I'd met Anne. I used to get nightmares about "hope'.

I can remember this one dream that I had, where I was on this carousel, sitting on a dark brown horse; I was the only one on the ride and I looked about three or four years old. My old man, better known as my father, was standing by the rail, watching me. I was scared to death because the damn thing kept getting faster and faster. Then I started to slide off. As my bum edged its way over the side of the saddle, I screamed, and clawed frantically at the plastic fur around the horse's neck. But my hands couldn't grasp anything, so I just kept sliding. Every time I went past my old man, I could hear him laughing hysterically. All I could do was continue to slide and scream. I went by my dad seventeen times and all he did was laugh-- uncontrollably. By the eighteenth time around, only my arms and hands were in contact with the plastic-casted creature. I couldn't see my dad anymore, but I could still hear his belly laughter. Then I heard him say, "Catch up with me, Mary. You can't do it, can you? You can't catch up with me." And then I fell. And his laughing stopped.

And the carousel stopped. And I'd wake up--crying.

There were other things too; but I don't want to bore you with my life story. I just didn't acknowledge the word "hope"; that's all.

Now, where was I with Anne? Oh yeah, I was at her funeral. She'd killed herself. The all-popular, ever fun-loving, Anne Kelso had pulled the plug to her own life support system, and she got away with it, too. I'd known she wasn't afraid to die; but I couldn't understand why she would want to leave a world that she seemed to love so much. That was beyond me--way beyond me. I mean, it was all right for me to hate the world. A person automatically hates something that hates them first, don't they? But the world seemed to love Anne and she seemed to love it back. I didn't understand how someone could leave something that they loved. Just because I didn't understand, didn't mean she didn't have good reasons though. I understand *that*.

Anyway, I was sitting alone in the back pew of that church thinking about Tuesdays and Thursdays, and my mother. My mom died the day I was born. It was my birthday present--the best present I ever got. I sat there thinking of how my mom would have rocked me to sleep and read me bedtime stories. I could even see her face; she looked just like me--dirty-blonde, wavy hair and big brown eyes--but her smile was prettier, which made *her* look beautiful. I know she would've been--beautiful, I mean. She would've dressed me up real nice in frilly dresses and sent me off to kindergarten with a hug. She would've sat down and wiped the tears from my face after Billy Horton pushed me off the monkey-bars. And she would've told me all about this "period" stuff that happens once a month. And on Tuesdays and Thursdays, I would've brought Anne home for supper and mom would've liked her. And Anne would've liked my mom. That's what I was thinking while everyone else was wrapped up in worry over why Anne had done what she had done.

And then, all of a sudden, I got this awful urge to look up at the coffin. I couldn't see the body, but that didn't matter; the body wasn't Anne. It was just a covering she'd been issued to make her look like the rest of us. The part that mattered was her soul. And it was alive--really alive.

"Hi Mary."

Those words made me jump. And right then and there I was ready to scream. There was no one around me--not that close, anyway. Besides, I knew that voice, and it didn't belong to anyone who was breathing.

I looked wildly around, and I must've gasped or made some sort of noise, because a few people turned around and noticed me sitting there. It took me a couple of seconds to realize what had happened, but since I already knew she was still alive, I didn't waste time questioning it. I simply thought, "Hi Anne." How I knew we could communicate with our minds, I'm not sure; it was just a feeling. You'd have to experience it to understand.

"You knew, didn't you." I heard her say.

"I had a pretty good idea."

We carried on in silent conversation; I was smiling by this time and enjoying the company.

"I didn't mean to upset everyone," Anne said.

"Death is hard for people to accept."

"You're not having a problem."

"You're here." I could feel her smiling. "What's it like?" I asked her calmly. My fear had vanished and my heart was pounding with excitement.

"It's lonely."

I nodded in response to this and got a few odd stares from some stragglers in the aisle.

"I deserve to know how you feel," she said.

I didn't know what to say to that one, so I kept my thoughts shut. I always said that if you're not sure what to say, then nothing's probably best.

"I can stay with you now. I can be with you for a while. If you want me to."

I looked around, trying to find her, to see her, but I couldn't. My heart got to beating even faster then, and I said, real foolish like, "What do you mean?"

"I can stay. I can come inside you...and stay. I can help you, Mary."

I couldn't believe it. Would you believe it? Well, I didn't. My eyes opened wide and I looked all around again. I got a few more odd stares.

"Forever?" I asked, stupidly.

"For a while."

I swallowed real hard then, and closed my eyes, wondering if it would hurt--can you imagine--and finally, not caring, my heart racing and my palms sweating, I clenched my fists and gave my head a forceful nod, "Okay, let's go for it."

I guess that was all she needed--my permission-- because a warm sensation tingled my arms and legs, reaching out to all parts of my body; it even tickled my eye-lids and made them twitch.

I guess I looked pretty foolish, sitting in the back pew at a funeral, my body tense, my eyes clamped shut, and big grin across my stupid face.

"Hey, are you okay?"

I jumped at the sound of the deep voice and opened my eyes. I turned my head and stared at a big guy with blue eyes and red, red hair. I pulled my eyes away from his and looked around, suddenly aware of where I was and why I was there. There were a lot of people staring at me. I'd stolen their attention away from the corpse and I found *that* incredibly funny, so I started laughing. When I find something funny, I laugh. It never happens very often, so I never learned how to control it. And man, did I laugh. Then the big guy with the red-delicious-apple-top hair grabbed my arm.

"Who the hell are you?" he yelled.

I looked around again. Now, everyone was looking at us. I laughed so hard that I couldn't catch my breath and my side hurt like hell.

"Mary-Anne," I yelled, "I'm Mary-Anne." And I ran like hell, leaving behind a lot of open mouths, but no open minds. I pushed at the heavy oak door and rushed out into the fresh air--I was still laughing--and gasped for breath. The hail had been replaced by gigantic snowflakes and Anne made me smile at them. I hated the snow; Anne liked it. After about ten minutes, I liked it too.

"Let's make an angel," Anne said excitedly.

"An angel?" I asked, wondering what she was talking about. But before I got an answer, I was lying in the snow on the boulevard, and flapping my arms and spreading my legs, pushing the snow into wings. Finally the creation was finished and we stood looking at it and smiling. I'd never made an angel before. A cold shiver of joy and excitement travelled through my body, and it was then that I realized that *this* was the world--the same world that had hated me--loving me. Me!

No, that wasn't the day I started going crazy; it was the day I stopped *being* crazy. My mind had been wrong for fifteen years; I had been wrong. My hate for the world had had nothing to do with what the world thought of me. All my anger and hatred had been based on my own imagination--unrealities.

For two years we did everything together. She taught me how to use the wind to fly a kite, how to bury myself in the sand and actually enjoy the coarseness of it as it clung to my body, how to listen to the birds in the spring, and how to enjoy the smell of chimney smoke on cold winter days.

Last week Anne spoke to me for the last time.

"I have to go now, Mary," she said.

"Where are we going?" I asked. I mean, we hadn't been separated for two years. But, even as I said it, I understood what she meant. I didn't want to understand, but I did.

We were looking out the kitchen window, watching the sun disappear slowly behind the bare trees. The sight was awesome.

"There's only one way you can come with me," she said.

The sky stared at us, glowing crimson between the trees. "I want your world, Anne. I want your world."

Darkness seemed to cave in soon after I said that. The trees looked hauntingly at me through the darkness; they were against me. With the sun went the beauty and the love; they dropped over the edge of the world. And so did Anne; I was alone again. I can't hope to be happy here alone; I just don't belong in this world. Anybody out there understand?

Robots

Maybe if it had happened a week ago or a week ahead, it would've been okay. But, it didn't; it happened today.

The bus...it's so crowded. Bodies are slamming against each other. The driving force is a confused foot. I think about the foot: *toes poke up through the sand; Tommy just finished burying me; he forgot my head, though; my head and my toes are too near the air; they are staring at me; accusing; I wonder what I did; suddenly, I can't stand it anymore; my head can still see what's going on; if my head can see, it doesn't do the rest of me any good.*

I start breathing hard. Right there. Flattened between people--robots.

Then I remember a story my dad told me about those

things. You push a button and they walk, serve, dance.

Another button and you can make it talk; a crackled kind of

voice that doesn't sound real--programmed. If the robot

doesn't do what you want it to do, you can take a panel off

of its back--a skin graft--and rearrange some wires and

replace the metallic skin. You can only hope it responds.

My back starts to ache; I'm still breathing hard. A

fat slob--he must be two hundred and fifty pounds, his shirt

hanging out over his pants, the buttons popped open--is

throwing an acrid smell into the air; he has greasy hair and

bucked teeth. My head makes contact with his shoulder

and he shoves me away. My back hits the bar you're

supposed to hang on to, and knocks my breath into the

faces--masks. Last Hallowe'en: *my little brother is going*

out as bugs bunny; he likes the face-mask the best, and he

keeps wanting me to put a mask on; I tell him I'll smile; he

doesn't understand; he's only four.

The confused foot hits the brake, and I bump into a little girl--she's holding her mother's hand. The old lady-- she looks twenty-five, which is old when you're only fifteen--gives me a dirty look, slanting her eyes and the whole bit. I wonder who pushes *her* buttons. She pulls the little girl closer to her. I grab the bar my back hit. Then, I remember my dad saying prisoners do that all the time; they try pushing their faces into the narrow slots. One guy bruised his cheeks doing it. The bar is cold against my cheek; it feels kinda good, which is okay, because the rest of me feels shitty. Then the foot hits the gas and the bar hits my cheek. The foot hits my cheek. It starts getting real sore and I feel sorry for the guy in jail. I want out just as bad as he does.

I can see the light above the rear door, but I can't see the door. The light is something; it's a destination. There's no point propelling myself between these machines if I don't think there's a way out. My breathing gets heavier. I clutch the bar, panicking--I can't fly. Dad flew once: *he jumps off a cliff with man-made wings--the cliff doesn't have wings, my dad does; if the cliff had wings, maybe my mom would fly too; she's scared; I'm not made yet; the ovens not warm enough.*

Now, I wonder what he did with those wings. Maybe he'll let me try it. I needed them today. Maybe if I tell my dad I wanna learn how to fly, he won't get so mad at me when he gets here. And mad, he is going to be. He'll have to pay for the damages, plus there's the medical bill; but, I guess O.H.I.P. will pay for that--if they pay for rooms in hospitals with bars on the windows.
I'm staring at the light like the captain of a ship stares at a lighthouse; I remember Peggy's cove: *I can't believe all the seagulls; they fly; they drop crap all over the place; I'm afraid to go outside, so I stay in the souvenir shop and look at the postcards; I don't need to be here; my folks could*

bring those pictures back and show them to me; a picture

of a seagull can't shit on you; then I wonder what would

happen if a whole bunch of them got together and crapped

all over the lighthouse, so the captain couldn't see the

light; it would look like a white blanket; but, it wouldn't

blow away. It isn't a lighthouse; it's the light over the door

in the bus and I gasp because I'm afraid something's gonna

cover it, or it'll disappear, or...something. I won't be sure

of a way out.

Someone bangs into me. It's the lady with the little

girl. I stare her down, and then smile at the kid. It's not the

kid's fault.

Kids always have to be with their mothers or their fathers.

The lady isn't too happy that I smiled at her kid, but I don't

care. I look back up at the light; it isn't glowing; that's

because the bus is moving. I let out some of the air I've

been holding prisoner--it isn't right that everything should

be locked up. Windows, closets, and doors should be
locked, but not air. I wait, breathing heavily, until the bus
breaths again. I wish it would breath more often; every
time it breaths, the light comes on. I start getting excited
about the position of the confused foot. That is the
dictator.

The big slob struggles between two skinny people,
taking away their air until he's through, then there's a whole
lot of air for everyone. The dictator announces breathing
time and spits out the fat robot. The sea gull misses the
light. I'm grateful. I can almost see the door. If I could
see the door, I wouldn't need the light anymore. I'm going
to move closer to it, but the robot with the kid gets pushed
into the space. An old guy takes their place.

I glance at the lighthouse. We aren't breathing
anymore. My cheek throbs and my head joins the band.
I'm wishing headaches came with softer music. I look at

the old man beside me. I look at his eyes, because he's not interested in mine. He's staring at the floor--at the feet. The floor on this bus is made out of feet. I wonder if he notices--probably not. He lets air out through his nose, and then opens his mouth; his lips flap against the flow of air as it's captured, then he closes his mouth and breaths out his nose again. Every time he does it, a grunt escapes; it isn't loud--probably I'm the only one who hears it. If I was sitting down, I'd give him my seat; but, since I'm part of the floor, I just move a little towards the back and give him more air. Not that I can afford it; there isn't much floating around. If someone offered me a hundred dollars for my air, I wouldn't sell; but this old guy is scaring me.

I look back up at the light. It still isn't time. I think the old man is gonna pass out. Then the dictator demands breathing time and the old guy lands on some lady's lap. I'm torn between my light and the poor wrinkled geezer.

I'm afraid he's gonna die; but, the lady's real nice and helps him up. He nods at her. I seek the lighthouse; it's gone again. If I was really a captain of a ship, I'd want my light to come on more often than this one does. I start to panic. I think the old guy isn't steerin' his boat too well; and, since the lighthouse isn't too trustworthy, I think he's gonna crash into me. Every time the light goes off, he comes my way. What if he crashes into me and dies? What if we both die?

Tommy's dead. He gets mad as hell at me for calling him Tommy. I don't know him when he's Tom, so I call him Tommy.

I don't think he should change his name because he's sixteen.

Mine'll still be Brian. Besides, I liked Tommy better than Tom. But when Tom dies, he takes Tommy with him. I don't think that's fair. My dad tells me to grow up; that I'm fifteen years old and I should start acting like it. Then, he hugs me. I don't know why; he just does it, right there at the funeral, with all his friends, and all my friends around. He even gets water in his eyes; how he does that, I don't know. All he says, is that 'death stings'. So, I'm scared, because I don't want to sting, and this old guy keeps getting closer to me, and he looks like he's gonna sting any minute.

Tommy doesn't look like he stings. He just looks like he's sleeping. And he isn't having a bad dream or anything, because he doesn't move. You don't have to breathe when you're dead.

I guess I could handle being dead in this bus, if it wasn't for the stinging part. My head, cheek, and back already ache. I don't need any stinging going on.

A bee sting is bad: *Tommy and I are up at his cottage; Tommy jumps off the dock and into the water before it can get him; but, I'm too slow; I always have to get my toes wet first, and the bee doesn't feel like waiting around; it gets me in the back, just as I'm sliding in; I slide too fast and the water splashes; little waves float away from me; Tommy's laughing; I never make waves; I don't like to disturb the water; I don't think I'd like people hitting, splitting, and messing my surface up if I was water; the welt on my back stings for two days.* But, Tommy doesn't look red and ugly. Maybe death has a different kind of sting. Either way I don't want to find out. I squish real close to the guy behind me. I'm gonna jump oughta the way before I get killed.

But, back this far, I can't see the light real well. In fact, I can't see it at all.

A green glow surrounds the head of the lady with the kid, and then it's gone. Is she an angel? I blink my eyes; they have deceived me before. Robots can't be angels. Angels are dead. Maybe Tommy's an angel. Does it sting to be a robot? Is the bus going to breathe again? I don't think so. The robot's head glows and the bus breaths; I sigh, attaching a moan to the escape of air. When do I get off?

How do I get ought of here? The dictator jerks the bus forward. The old man...I don't waste any time. I throw my bag of books at the window.

A lady screams. My ears ring. I'm going deaf. My books land on someone's lap. I grab them. The window is still there--locked. The old man...I heave them again and again! He touches me! Death touches me! I scream and hurl myself behind my books. The dictator brakes. Glass shatters. I breathe. All the way down, I breathe. Like drowning backwards. So much air, I don't know what to do with it.

I think I could share it with the robots in the bus. But robots don't need air; they don't need lights; they don't have to learn how to steer their ships. Someone else does it. Who? I wonder as my body skids against the ground. Tires screech, numbing my ears. I can't hear. I'm going deaf.

My back stings. I know I'm dying. Robots don't die. Now, I

     know I'm not a robot. Tom says I'm a robot. He says he's

     going to kill himself because he's a robot. But he isn't a

     robot. He's wrong. I start crying.

          Maybe it would've been better if we'd both been

     robots. We wouldn't have had to cry. He wouldn't have

     died.

Second Chance

Sara looked around. Several girls were watching television in a room to the right of the foyer she had just entered. Stairs rose on her left; and straight ahead, voices came from the kitchen.

"Jesus Christ, Laurie, if you really believe him, go. Get the hell ought of here."

Sara looked at Cheryl, who shrugged and motioned her forward. A short girl with blonde hair rushed past them and hurried up the stairs.

A woman was standing with her back to them, leaning over the kitchen sink. "Damn," she muttered and shattered a glass into the sink.

"Marcy?" Cheryl said softly, "everything okay?"

The woman turned around and pushed some grey-black hair away from her face. Dark circles surrounded the grey eyes, and wrinkles edged away from the corners of her eyes and lips. "Cheryl, sweetie?" she said gently, "who's your friend?" She wiped her hands on the towel which was flung over the cupboard door below the sink.

"Sara. I met her downtown. She's looking for a place to stay."

Marcy looked carefully at Sara, "How old are you?" she asked.

Sara glanced at Cheryl and pulled instinctively away from the hand that was slowly approaching her chin.

"Sixteen," Sara said. The approaching hand fell back to rest in its partner. Sara stared at them. They were wrinkled with age.

"Well," Marcy turned back towards the sink, "Laurie should have her stuff out soon. Why don't you have something to eat? Cheryl will show you to the room later."

The broken glass clattered against the stainless-steel sink, making Sara's teeth hurt.

"Okay. Thanks." Sara said.

"There are meat pies in the freezer, Cheryl. Heat up a few. You both look hungry," Marcy dropped the broken glass into the garbage. "Stay and keep her company tonight, Cheryl, and make sure she sees Deana when she gets here." Marcy paused and looked at Sara, "Have a seat, sweetie. You look tired. Travelling takes a lot out of you. Where're ya from?"

Sara sat down on an old wooden chair--one of the five surrounding the table. "Windsor," she said softly.

Cheryl put the meat pies in the oven and sat down opposite Sara, "she's been on the road for a week, sleeping in wrecked cars and garage bathrooms."

"A week?" Marcy said as she finished up the dishes, "That's a long time just from Windsor."

"She had trouble getting a ride from London, and she's been here, in Toronto, for two days." Cheryl said.

"You should let the girl speak for herself, Cheryl. You won't be around when Deana questions her."

Cheryl lit up a cigarette and offered one to Sara who refused it. The buzzer on the oven went off several minutes later and Marcy served them each two beef pies. Sara accepted them graciously. She hadn't eaten in two days and even though the pies were under-cooked, her stomach welcomed them.

The bedroom was pleasant; dressed in pink and burgundy, it had a rich feel to it. Sara laid her knap-sack on the bed that was bare of all belongings. A real bed, she thought, she hadn't thought she would ever sleep in one again. She smiled at Cheryl, who had entered the room with her and who was now shuffling a deck of cards.

"Who's Deana?" Sara asked after several minutes of silence.

Cheryl sat on the floor between the twin beds and motioned for Sara to do the same. Sara sat down, with her legs crossed, opposite Cheryl.

"She's kinda the boss around here." Cheryl answered.

"Who's Marcy then?" Sara asked, wondering how many questions she could get away with.

"Well, she's the big boss, but she's getting older now and doesn't want to deal with us too much. Deana'll take over when Marcy's washed-up."

Sara nodded, and Cheryl dealt the cards.

"Gin rummy," Cheryl said, "you know how to play?"

Sara nodded. "How come I have to see her?"

"Everybody has to see her. She's the one that decides if we can stay. Aces are wild." Cheryl said

"That's wild rummy," Sara said.

"Well, we're playing that, then."

They played a couple of hands in silence. Cheryl was winning.

"What's Deana like?" Sara asked, looking at her cards.

Cheryl shrugged and picked up a card from the deck, "She's really pretty, and knows how to dress well; but she's a little rough. She doesn't have a lot of sympathy behind her attractive appearance."

"Think she'll let me stay?" Sara asked.

Cheryl laid her cards down, "I'm out again. Yeah she'll let you stay. I've only seen her turn a couple of girls away, and they were really young."

"She just turned them onto the street?"

Cheryl laughed and shuffled the cards, "Like I said. She's not a very warm person."

Two days went by and Sara had only heard of the existence of Deana.

Everything Cheryl had told her had been backed up by the other girls; Sara found herself feeling both frightened and intrigued by the mention of Deana's name. During those two days, Sara's thoughts about her surroundings had been confirmed. Nobody was around at night; everybody slept during the day. She'd given it a lot of thought and had decided that she could sleep with anybody, now. Nothing could be as bad as entertaining your own father.

Sara was laying on her bed when a knock on the door startled her. She sat up and swung her legs over the side of the bed, "Come in."

The door opened and a woman entered. Sarah's eyes widened in surprise and she stared at the beautiful brown hair and big brown eyes. The nose was in perfect proportion to the eyes and mouth; very little make-up enhanced the beauty. Sara smiled, sure that no one that beautiful could be a monster inside.

"You're Sara?" the woman asked.

Sara nodded.

"Is your voice on vacation?" the stranger demanded.

"No, I'm sorry." Sara's voice was barely audible.

"I'm Deana. I'm sure you've heard enough about me to know that I'm not a very patient person. So please answer my questions quickly and audibly."

"Yes, Mam," Sara said politely. She watched as Deana took a seat on the other bed.

"How old are you?" Deana asked.

Sara hesitated, "Sixteen."

Deana's eyes flames with rage, "I don't tolerate lying. You will leave in the morning." She rose to leave.

Sara looked wildly at her, water was pushing through her eyes, and her heart beat furiously, "Wait! I'm sorry. I'll tell you the truth." She bent down and pulled her knapsack out from under the bed, her hands fumbled through it. "Here's my birth certificate. I'll be sixteen in August."

Deana stood with her hand on the doorknob. She turned to look at Sara. Her eyes showed shock and surprise; the ice seemed to melt immediately and a warmth glowed through. She walked back to the bed, taking Sara's birth certificate from the out-stretched hand, before sitting down.

Sara sat silently, rubbing her sweaty hands together.

"Marcy told me you were from Windsor. Why does this say you were born in Toronto? Did your parents move?"

Sara looked momentarily at Deana and then pulled her eyes away, "I was adopted."

"As a baby?" Deana asked, her voice quivering slightly.

"I was a couple of months old."

Deana stared at her for a long time. Sara thought she looked nervous; she was licking her lips nervously. Sara wondered what was wrong.

The strict harshness of Deana's voice had disappeared and she was asking the questions sensitively.

"Your name was Sara before you were adopted?" Deana stood up and paced the room.

"Yes."

"They didn't change your name?" Deana asked.

"No. They liked Sara."

Deana smiled and sat back down on the bed. "Why did you run away?"

Sara looked away and played with her hands again, "I didn't like it there."

"And the grass is greener here, is it?" Deana's sensitivity fled and a sarcastic tone took its place.

Sara looked up at Deana, her bottom lip quivering.

Deana suddenly stood up, "I want to talk to you again, later." She handed the birth certificate back to Sara; she moved her hand towards Sara's chin, but drew it back just as Sara turned her head away. She left without another word.

After staring at the ceiling for what seemed to be an hour, Sara fell asleep. She missed supper and the hard knock on her door.

"Sara...Sara." Cheryl's voice drifted into her dream.

"Wha-what?" Sara's eyes opened and she looked around the room before focusing on Cheryl, "What is it?"

"Deana wants to see you in her room. She's been acting really strange this evening...hasn't said 'boo' to anyone.'

Sara had jumped off the bed and was pulling a brush through her hair, "Where's her room?" she asked and headed for the door.

"It's the last one on the left, at the end of the hall." Cheryl said as Sara slipped out the door, "Good-luck."

Sara turned back and smiled, "Thanks." She walked quickly down the hall and knocked on the door Cheryl had pointed out.

"What?" a voice snapped.

"Cheryl said you wanted to see me." Sara spoke nervously.

"Yes, Sara. Come in," the voice returned softly.

Sara opened the door and stepped into a dimly lit room. The only light was a small reading lamp on the dresser near where Deana was standing, staring at a framed picture. She looked up and smiled weakly when Sara entered.

"Have a seat in the rocking chair, Sara. I have some questions, and I want straight answers." She spoke evenly, but without bitterness.

Sara obeyed and sat down.

"Why aren't you at home?" Deana asked softly. "What happened that made you leave?"

Sara looked down at the floor and rocked the chair nervously.

"Damn it Sara, tell me!" Deana demanded. "What the hell did they do to you?" she yelled, and approached Sara, who had stopped rocking and had stood up.

Deana's voice broke and she grabbed for Sara as if she was going to shake her, but Sara ducked away with expertise.

Sara stood with her back against the door and hand on the doorknob. She was confused by the emotion that Deana showed. She'd been told that Deana was made of stone--no emotion, no feeling.

Deana backed away from her. "They beat you, didn't they? I can tell by the way you just jumped out of my way. Marcy told me you wouldn't let her touch you either. And today, in your room, if I hadn't pulled away, you would have." Deana sat down on the bed as if she was defeated, "Tell me Sara. I've heard the worst horror stories. You can't shock me."

Sara took her hand off of the doorknob, but stayed by the door. "Look, maybe it wasn't that bad. You know how teenagers exaggerate sometimes." She looked at Deana, who was staring vacantly back at her.

"Sara, do you know what the girls do here?"

Sara nodded, staring down at her feet.

"And you can do what they do?"

Sara squeezed her hands together, "I think so."

"Have you had sex before?' Deana asked quietly.

Sara pulled her arms tight around her body and squeezed her eyes shut to force back the tears.

"If you're willing to sleep with anybody, just to be away from home, then it had to be pretty bad."

Sara slid her back down the door to the floor, and drew her knees to her chest with her arms, "He...he used to beat me when I was small," Sara stammered. "I grew up in hospitals--a different one every time," she paused and wiped harshly at the tears that were streaming down her cheeks. "When I got older, say three or four years ago, he...he..." Sara broke into sobs, unable to continue.

Deana drew closer, and sat on the floor opposite Sara, "He made you sleep with him, didn't he?"

Sara nodded, biting her lip, sniffling, and wiping away the tears, all at the same time.

Deana pushed the hair out of Sara's face. Sara withdrew and rose nervously to her feet. She smiled weakly, "I'm sorry. I'd better go."

Dianne watched her fumble for the doorknob, "You can stay Sara."

Sara looked at Deana and nodded, "Thanks," she said weakly, and disappeared out the door.

"Damn it Deana, she's been here for two weeks and you haven't set her up yet. The other girls are asking questions. They're starting to hate her."

There was silence. Sara stood at the bottom of the stairs and listened to the voices as they travelled from the kitchen.

"She's so cold, Marcy. She's just like me, but she's eighteen years younger. I should never have let her go. I did this to her."

Deana's words drifted to Sara's ears; she sat down on the bottom step and grasped the vertical wooden bars of the banister. Tears welled up in her eyes.

"She might not be yours, Deana. You don't know for sure."

"I do, Marcy. She has a birthmark behind her left ear, just like Peter's; and she looks like him." Deana paused briefly, then went on, "I gave her up because I loved her, remember. I wanted the best for her. Look what she got stuck with. Damn those social workers!" Deana's voice quivered, "She would've been better off with a hooker for a mother."

Silence hovered in the air and Sara stood up, ready to go back upstairs. But Marcy's voice halted her movement; she leaned closer to the kitchen.

"If you still love her, tell her. You've melted because of her. She's not too old to melt, too. But get her out of here for Christ's sake; it's not doing her any good having the other girls hate her."

"Where will we go? What will I do?" Deana's voice pleaded in question.

"Get your own apartment. Get a proper job. You're a lot older now. You can make the adjustment." Marcy said softly.

Sara ran up the stairs, leaving audible footsteps in her wake. She bounded down the hall and flung open the door to Deana's room. The picture was still on the dresser and she grabbed it. She stared for a long time at her father and mother. Tears dropped onto the photograph; she wiped them off.

"I guess I have some explaining to do."

The voice startled Sara. She looked into Deana's tear-glazed eyes and then back down at the picture. When she looked up again, Deana was almost beside her. Sara moved towards her and accepted the embrace. She cried in loud sobs and pressed her eyes against Deana's shoulder.

Deana kissed the top of Sara's head and pushed the hair out of her daughter's face. "We'll get out of here, Sara. . And we'll make it. Just the two of us."

The Bird

In the dream she can see the birds--seagulls, they are--through the mist, looping back and forth above the waves that crash against the rocks. Their wings spread wide, their beaks opening and closing with each squawk. Two fly off together. They seem to come and go as they please. A heavy wave hits the rock and the birds scatter. When she wakes up she doesn't know where she is.

She moves her arms--up and down. The sleeves of the gown are tied behind her back, her ankles braced together. She bends her knees and tries to pull to a sitting position, but falls back, cramping her stomach muscles. Four walls, four corners, a ceiling, a floor--all white. *Where am I?*

Her body gives an involuntary shudder. Sweat seeps from her top lip, followed by beads on her forehead. She twists and turns, but she can't escape. She turns onto her stomach and squirms in discomfort.

Something scrapes and clicks beyond her feet. She twists onto her side and curls towards the noise. A panel with a window opens inward, declaring its thickness. She stares at the three strangers as they enter the room.

"You're awake." The low female voice echoes off the walls and she follows the echoes with her eyes, twisting her neck. The gown is stuck to her back and dampness seeps through under both of her arms. She clenches her teeth and stares at the woman. A long blue sweater hangs to her thighs and is unbuttoned, exposing jeans and a sweat-shirt. Dark brown hair falls in waves to just past her shoulders, parted at the side and swept across her forehead. The body steps closer.

"What's your name?" The woman asks gently.

She remains silent and still, and stares beyond the open door.

The woman follows her stare and motions for the two men who had accompanied her to leave. They close the door behind them.

"My name's Torey," the woman says. "What can I call you?"

She stares at the woman for several moments, pulling at her arms, trying to free herself. She rolls onto her back--exhausted.

"Jaime." She said and looks hopefully at Torey, "Can you get me out of this?"

"How do you feel?"

Scared. She watches the woman, "Claustrophobic. How would you feel?"

Torey smiles and moves closer to Jaime, bending down onto one knee beside her. "Okay, roll onto your side."

Jaime feels the cotton loosen at her elbows as the pressure ceases. She pulls her arms out quickly and rubs her hands together, then stretches them out, away from her body and as far from each other as she can get them.

"My feet?" she asks, sitting up.

Torey smiles, "Stretch them out here."

Torey unfastens the buckle and loosens the strap. It slides over her feet. Jaime rubs her ankles and stands up unsteadily. She walks around the room, wind-milling her arms and taking in the sterile air.

"What's your last name Jaime?"

Jaime looks at her for a moment. *They don't know who I am.* She paces the room, her arms swinging from front to back. *I can be anyone now.* She holds her arms high in the air and bends to touch her toes. She twists her neck from that position and looks at Torey, "Somers." She laughs.

Torey smiles and glances down at the floor. She crosses her arms in front of her. "I can come back later. Think you'll feel like talking after another few hours in here?"

Jaime stands up straight and bites the inside of her lip; she hugs herself and then quickly drops her arms to her sides. "You win." She turns away and walks to the far right corner. "What do you already know?" She draws a circle with her big toe on the cold floor. *They're going to send me back.* The hair on her body crawls.

"That you were flying on L.S.D. two nights ago and thought the Grand River looked inviting, since Niagara Falls was so far away." Torey moves closer, "My guess is you're between twenty and twenty-five, weigh 125 pounds and stand 5'6" tall."

"Twenty-two...5'6 1/2"...130 pounds...but you did pretty good." Jaime looks at Torey, "That's it? You really don't know my name?"

Torey shakes her head, "All you possessed was a desire to fly and the clothes you're wearing."

Jaime presses her back against the corner and slides down to the floor, her legs wrapped within her arms and drawn to her chest. She bites her jeans at the knee.

"We have to contact your parents or relatives. They'll be wondering where you are."

Jaime gnaws at the denim, staring blankly into space. *They'll be wondering where my rings are, but they won't be wondering about me. The corvette can stay in the garage. The marble sinks and oak staircase will still exist without me there. All the fine grain furniture and polished tables will still shine without me looking into them. The pool balls can be racked up and shot at without me doing it.*

She could see herself in her own room, staring out the window. *She watches the birds circle the tree before landing on its branches.*

"Jaime."

She cringes at the sound of her mother's shrill voice. A bang on the door and the knob turns. It creaks open.

"What are you doing up here, honey? Tom's down stairs. He says he's been ringing the doorbell for fifteen minutes. He wants you to go for a drive with him." Her mother picks up a shirt from the chair and hangs it in the closet, straightens up the dresser, and smooths down the comforter on the queen-sized bed.

Her eyes follow the movements of her mother. "You mean he wants to go for a drive with me."

"Whatever, dear. He's a fine young man. You want to marry someone like him. Now hurry up. Don't keep him waiting."

She stands up slowly. "Did you have a good trip?" She asks softly.

"Of course, Hun. But two weeks isn't long enough. Now stop wasting time and get down there."

She slouches past her mother, towards the door; she turns when she reaches the archway, and her lips part, but they close without a sound, and she goes down the stairs.

Tom is pacing the living room, cracking his knuckles; he runs to the front door when he sees her, and opens it for her. She stares at him. He smiles, revealing his perfect white teeth.

As they make their way to the shiny red car, he asks "Where're the keys?"

She drops them into his hand, and slumps into the front seat.

"Maniac time," he says, and revs the engine.

She glances at him, sighs, and stares out the side window.

"When's your old man get back?"

"Dun no." Don't care. Wish he would stay away
forever. The corvette whizzes past the speed limit cars on
the highway.

"Your old lady's pretty cool, eh?"

She watches the broken white lines on the road.

"She invited me for supper tonight."

She looks at him, "Just you and her, eh?"

He smiles, "Of course not. You'll be there."

"I have plans."

"Change 'em. It's your mother's first day back.
You owe her one night of your life, at least."

She chews the inside of her cheek, clamping down
tight. She watches the broken white lines, and remembers
the birds in her dream last night, flapping their wings and
squawking at the edge of the cage.

"Jaime? Are you okay?" The soft voice brings her
back to the present.

She licks her lips and wipes the tears off of her cheek with the back of her hand. "I don't want them to know I'm here."

Torey sighs and sits down beside her. "You'll have to stay here longer if there's no-one out there who can help."

Jaime nods.

"There's no-one you want to get a hold of?"

"No-one."

"Okay. But let me know if you change your mind."

"I won't change my mind."

Torey stood up, "Come on then. Let's find you a half-decent room."

The room is small with two hospital beds--the right one cluttered with books and clothes--a small desk and chair, and a dresser. The hair on her arms tingles and rises.

She hurries to the bed on the left-hand side of the room, lays down, and falls asleep. In the dream she is perched on the rock, the lake breeze taking away her breath, the splashing waves showering her body, watching the birds come and go as they pleased.

Things Change

He runs across the tracks, down the gully, bending through the tunnel, his hands, knees, and toes brushing the cement, back to his feet, through the corn stalks, the fresh corn smell, the cabin roof visible, the top of the door, the window; the uneven walkway trips him up, his nose bleeds against the cement, he gets up, running, past the well, turning the doorknob, stumbling up the step, slamming the splintered door, he presses his back against it, looking as if he were more afraid of what was inside than of what was outside.

"Did you get it?"

He stares at the other boys, licks the blood from his lip and chin, and smiles.

"Of course." He pulls the brown paper bag out of his jacket and drops to his knees between the two boys.

"Give it here Bobby."

"Get out Sam." He pushes Sam's arm away, "I got it. I'll look after it."

"That wasn't the deal."

"Shut-up, Chris." He opens the bag and stares inside. "It's the deal now."

It lay on its side, the trigger ready, waiting for his finger. He holds his breath and lifts the black gun. It lay flat in his hand.

"Wow."

"Did they see you?"

He touches it with the fingers of his other hand. Running the tips along the barrel, over the chamber and down to the trigger. He runs his finger back and forth along the curve. Blood drips onto his hand; he pulls it away from the gun. "Get me something for my nose."

Sam grabs for the gun. Bobby knocks his hand away and stands up, fumbling with the gun, holding it in both hands. He aims at Sam. "Get me something for my nose."

Sam jumps backwards, knocking over the chair.

"Bobby!"

"Shut-up." He switches the aim to Chris. "Sam," he looks at Chris, "Get me something for my nose."

Sam moves in the corner of his eye, towards the table, he turns to watch. He feels his knuckles crush and watches the gun fly past him, whopping to the floor.

Chris dives for it, through the dust, rushing for the handle.

Bobby stares into the open end; he wipes his nose with the back of his hand and licks his lips. The blood is nearly dry.

"Give him the cloth, Sam."

Bobby takes the cloth, looks back at Chris, at the gun, and slams out the door. He dunks the rag into the flower pot of rain water and washes his face. The door squeaks open.

"Did anyone see you?"

Bobby smiles.

Chris nods and smiles back. "Come on. We've gotta work this out."

He follows Chris inside. They sit on the floor, legs crossed, gun in the middle, where they all stare.

"No one gets the gun," Chris said. "Not until we're ready." He looks at Bobby. "Okay?"

Bobby wonders if it was always so shiny. "Yeah." His grandfather had kept it shiny; he wondered who kept it shiny now? His father didn't have time and his mother hated it. It must have always been shiny; his grandfather had wasted his time.

"But I won't waste mine."

"Waste what? We're not gonna waste anybody. We're just gonna scare 'em a little."

Bobby looks at Chris, at Sam; they are glaring back; he looks at the gun.

"I gotta go." Sam stood and brushed the seat of his pants.

"It's only nine o'clock."

Bobby stares at the gun. He had killed for that gun. No. That was something else. Not killing. Not killing exactly. Something else.

"Why Bobby? Why?"

"He asked me to."

"What?"

He looks up. The two boys are staring at him. Chris bends down and picks up the gun.

"We're going."

"Where?"

"Home." Chris puts the gun in the paper bag. "I'm hiding it under the blanket."

"Someone might find it."

"No one comes here but us."

Bobby stands and holds out his hand. "I'll hide it."

"Where?"

"Yeah, where?" Sam stepped closer to Bobby.

"There's been cigarette butts around here."

"That's just Jeff."

"No one comes here but us," Bobby mocks.

"Jeff doesn't count."

Bobby steps closer to Chris, brushing jackets, "Jeff counts. Give me the gun."

Chris stares back at him, blinking; Bobby dares defiance. Sam takes a step backwards. Chris remains calm and smiles.

"You don't have to get so angry. It's your gun. Just make sure we can find it again. He hands the paper bag

over and chucks him on the shoulder, "You were lookin'
like my dad for a minute there." Chris nudges Sam
towards the door, "You comin'?"

Bobby watches the door open, feels the breeze slip
in. He relaxes and smiles, "No. I'm gonna hide this and
stick around."

"Okay, see ya tomorrow." Chris pulls the door shut
behind him.

Bobby looks at the paper bag and goes to the
window. He rubs the dirt with his fingers, squeaking the
glass, and watches them disappear into the corn. The sun
is touching the ground; it looks as if you could run to it,
touch it, and go down with it to wherever it went. The
world is funny that way, making things that were
impossible look possible.

He lights the lantern on the table, and pulls the gun
out, setting the bag down; he sits on the floor beside the

rotting fireplace. He grasps the handle, his finger on the trigger, raising the nose with his other hand, his head cocked to one side, right eye closed, aiming at the door-knob, and pulls the trigger. It doesn't fire. The trigger won't pull back. He lowers it and turns the chamber; it clicks and pings; he turns it again, looking in at the emptied holes. Bullets. He's forgotten about the bullets. The others hadn't asked. He turns the chamber, click-pinging, around and around. He remembers the hammer and pulls it back, aims at the door-knob again and pulls the trigger; it clicks and the hammer springs back into place. He does it again and again.

His grandfather let him play with it like this, years ago, when he was seven or eight. And later when he'd turned ten he got to shoot a real bullet, but only one. At a tin can, set on a decaying tree up by the fishing lake.

He pulls the bullets, noticing their warmth, out of his coat pocket. A whole handful. The window is dark now; he will have to wait until morning. He puts the bullets back.

He misses the summers with his grandfather, spent in the cabin, not much bigger than the one he sat in right now. If he cleaned it up...*"Cleanliness is next to Godliness in the city Bobby, but out here...out here you're as close as you can get."* His arm aches; he sets the gun on the floor beside him. It has been a cool day and the night is making it cooler. He gets the blanket, laying in the corner, wraps it around himself and sits back down on the cool wooden floor.

His father had been angry when he left. He is supposed to be grounded. "You're only thirteen years old young man, and while you live under my roof you'll do as I say."

But he had opened the door anyway.

"If you step out that door, you stay there. You hear me."

And he'd stepped out. What can his father do? He has his rights. They'd been taught that in school. He is a person and can do as he pleases...

"Your father loves you, Bobby."

"He doesn't even know me."

"He works hard."

"He's always yelling when he sees me."

"He wants you to grow up right."

"He hates me."

"He loves you. You're just a boy, ten years old; you're not old enough to do as you please."

But his grandfather was wrong; maybe he was wrong about everything. He pulls the bullets out of his pocket and counts them--fifteen.

He lays them beside the gun, and watches them... *"They're ruining the world, Bobby. Look, you can see the stacks of the factories from here." He followed his grandfather's pointing finger, across the lake, past the other farms. Black smoke grayed the sky. "Used to be farms for miles. The city's getting closer. Modern technology. Huh." His grandfather cracked a stick over his knee. "Don't let the selfishness of the world ever get you Bobby. I'm fifty-five years old and the land has always served me well enough. I don't need all those modern conveniences. I'm happier than your father who has everything."*

"We don't have a dishwasher."

His grandfather laughed and mussed his hair, "That's why they had you."

"I don't like doing dishes."

"Poor Bobby. Well, I'm afraid there'll be a lot of things you'll have to do that you won't like as you get older."

And there has been. Last year he'd had to start mowing the lawn and then just when he thought it was over the snow came and he'd had to shovel the driveway. How many more things would there be? Why is he here if he has to do what he hates? What is the point?

"Don't let the selfishness of the world ever get you Bobby."

"You did, damn it. You let it get to you. You and all your dumb ideas. Lies. They were all lies!" He feels the lump form at the back of his throat. He hasn't cried since...he hasn't cried in a long time. He cries now, "Damn you. You and your lies."

He picks up the gun and six bullets, snuffing his nose, gasping for breath; the blurred bullets fumble into the holes, he wipes his eyes, clear for a second, blurred again. His hands shake.

"Why'd you do it Bobby?"

"He asked me to."

"Why Bobby?"

He jumps up and spins around, the gun shaking at the abandoned blanket, "Shut up! Shut up!" He holds his hands over his ears, the gun--hard against his head--points at the ceiling. He gasps, his head throbs with the pain of tears and his nose runs.

All the psychologists, all the social workers, "He wants to be near the country," they said. And he did, but more than that he wanted someone to believe him.

"You said it would be okay," he yells at the ceiling, his hands hanging at his sides now, slowly turning around, his voice, thick with tears, rasps, "It's not okay. Liar! Liar! Liar!" His body heaves as the tears poor out. He gasps for breath. The door swings open. He stands, exhausted, the heavy gun at his side, his body heaving with each rasped breath.

"Get out." But the gun slips from his wet fingers and thuds to the floor. He drops down beside it.

"Bobby. What the hell--"

"He says, *'When they put me on one of those life machines,'*" Bobby draws in a quick breath, "*'you turn off the alarm button,'*" he gasps, "*'and pull the plug.'*" He has to push the words out. "*'I'm gonna die anyway,'* he said." He looks at the gun and touches it with his finger.

"Bobby. Don't--"

"I killed him!"

"He asked you to."

Jeff moves closer, his shadow from the lamp light touching Bobby's knees.

"Doesn't matter." He puts his finger in the hole by the trigger, the gun still flat on the floor, and runs it around and around.

"I jumped on top of him when they tried to save him, when the other alarm went off. The one he didn't tell me about. I held onto the sheets." His voice grows angrier, "I wouldn't let go. All the noise, the voices and that dumb bell, beeping and beeping." He lowers his voice and wipes his hand under his nose. "But no more pump and no more machine. When the doctor pulled us apart, I took the tube from his mouth with me." He lifts the gun, "I killed him."

Jeff's feet are beside him, then his knees, the buckles of the leather jacket clink against the floor. He feels the hand under his chin and looks into Jeff's eyes.

"You did the right thing Bobby. It's the rest of the world that's messed up." Jeff takes his hand away and stands up. "You're a mess."

He opens his mouth.

"Let's get you cleaned up and--"

He pulls the hammer back and clamps his teeth around the cold metal. The side of his mouth takes the blow--he hasn't pulled the trigger--and his jaw cracks, the gun is forced to rip out the other side. The blood rushes down his throat--he hasn't pulled the trigger--and he chokes and opens his eyes. He feels himself fall backwards, the room spinning, his stomach heaving, and darkness.

He is rocking. He opens his eyes and sees two pair of legs coming out from under him, his own and Jeff's. He recognizes the black cowboy boots and ripped faded jeans.

"Come on, kiddo."

He coughs and swallows blood.

"Bobby?"

He rocks back and forth, his arms being held tight in front of him, his head resting on Jeff's chest.

"Pretty close one, kid. Never been so scared before. Congratulations," Jeff pauses and loosens his grip.

"It's not the way to go. You don't escape by running away. This cabin. Death. I've got seven years on you. How can you feel this way already?"

Bobby stares at the feet. He puts his tongue into the large hole where his teeth had been and snatches it back, wincing in pain.

"It's the way the world is now Bobby, making you think you're older than you are, older than me, older than your grandfather ever was. They take away the innocence."

Bobby looks at the window. It is getting light, and the birds are making noise.

"You probably don't understand that." Jeff stops rocking, "Turn around and sit here." He taps the floor beside him.

Bobby moves. Every muscle aches.

"And I thought you were a mess before."

He opens his mouth, but it is too sore to speak.

"Yeah. I'll bet it hurts. Sorry about that, kiddo. See how sometimes we do things to help people even though it seems to hurt them. Like you and your grandpa."

Bobby looks at the floor. Jeff lifts his chin, making him flinch in pain.

"You don't still think you were wrong, do you?"

Bobby shrugs.

"Well," he lets his chin go, "you weren't. He was going to die; he just wanted to choose the time."

He stops talking. Bobby scans the floor.

"I've got it. It's mine until you're okay."

The door swings open. Chris and Sam storm in.

"Bobby.... Wow, what happened?" Sam sputters.

Jeff touches his elbow and helps him up. He stares out the door, at the field and the birds flying by. The corn wavers with the wind; it all seems to move at once.

"Where're you going?" Chris asks. Sam stares at Bobby's mouth.

"Home. That is where you guys should be."

"You haven't been home in over a year."

Jeff smiles and lights a cigarette. He slips off his jacket and puts it around Bobby. "Things change. Things change all the time."

"Dad hasn't changed," Chris says.

Bobby pulls the jacket tight around him. He can see the train going by at the end of the corn field.

"I have," Jeff says, and they slowly walk out.

Bobby looks back at the cabin, the two boys in the doorway, the broken walk. He turns around and walks quickly to catch up with Jeff in the middle of the corn field.

ONE WAY OUT

A Novella

PROLOGUE

The four friends moved about the interrogation room: Matt, twenty-five with blonde hair and green eyes, picked at the dirt under his fingernails; Aaron, twenty-six with brown hair and brown eyes, ran his fingers across the table...and back again; Stacey, with short red hair and green eyes, moved from one end of the room to the other, her arms hugging her body; and Kyle, the youngest of the four, tipped his chair back against a corner in the small room and rocked noiselessly.

The door clicked open and a female officer, identified as Detective Carson by the white badge attached to her civilian jacket, stepped in.

The four friends stopped all movement for a second and looked at her--she was smiling sympathetically--before resuming their previous activities.

Now, each of them stared down. Fingernails, a table top, the floor, and dangling feet, stared back. The presence of guilt, fear, anger, grief, and death was alive within these walls, and each of them felt it.

"Nicole left this note."

"Nikki." Matt whispered, still staring at his nails.

"Sorry. Nikki left this note. It's evidence and can't be taken from the precinct, but it's directed to the four of you so I thought you should see it."

Kyle dropped the chair onto all four legs and looked at Matt.

Aaron plopped onto one of the chairs, his elbows on the table; his head falling into his hands.

Stacey stopped pacing and sat on the floor, her back against the wall; she drew her knees to her chest.

Matt picked fiercely at his fingernails. His jaw was tight, restraining tears, out of anger or grief, he wasn't sure. He looked up at the officer. Her smile was gone, replaced by a sullenness that had captured all the faces within the room. He held out his hand and accepted the note, which he looked at in surprise, for it was not the type of note one would expect to be handed at a time like this; it was a whole pile of papers. Matt had to smile. Leave it to Nikki; she always did want to be a writer.

Matt looked at the others, his smile gone. He drew in a deep breath but didn't say anything; a lump had formed in his throat. He pulled out a chair, scratching its feet against the tiled floor, and sat across from Aaron at the table. Setting the pile of papers on the table, he looked at Kyle, his little brother; yet, not so little anymore, standing five feet ten inches, he was an inch taller than Matt; but they had the same blonde wavy hair, which, Matt had to admit, had attracted quite a few girls--including Nikki.

He looked back down at the pile of papers, and touched them gently.

He didn't know if he wanted to know why.

1

"Can we read this alone?" Matt asked the officer, still looking down at the papers in front of him.

"Sure." The officer turned to leave.

"Wait," Kyle broke in, "h-h-how long do we h-h-have?" forcing the words out painfully.

The officer turned back and smiled, "As long as you need. You can leave at any time and come back again if you want. Just check the papers in and out at the desk at the end of the hall."

She turned again and closed the door behind her.

"You gonna read it?" Stacey asked, looking at Matt.

Matt looked at each of them: Aaron glanced up and nodded, his face expressionless: Stacey, still hugging her knees on the floor, also nodded: Kyle shrugged, leaned back in his chair and folded his arms across his chest.

"Shit," Matt said, tapping the top page with his fingers, "Why the hell would she do this?"

"Why don't you read the damn thing and find out," Aaron snapped.

Matt looked at Aaron, staring straight through him.

"What the hell's the matter with you?" Aaron grabbed for the pile of papers, knocking the table with his thighs and banging it into Matt's chest.

Matt jumped up, knocking the table back into Aaron, grabbed the papers and threw them across the room; they scattered across the floor, "I don't wanna know what the fuck she did it for. She was messed up--obviously. Fucked-up. Completely fucked-up and none of us knew it."

Matt slammed out the door; but the others could see his silhouette--his back and head pressed against the door.

Stacey and Kyle began sorting through the pages, conveniently numbered, "Man, she had this planned for a long time," Kyle said. He looked up at Aaron who was watching them.   Aaron stepped towards Kyle and mussed his hair, "Yeah, she knew what she was doing, kiddo." He offered a weak smile and turned to see if Matt was still outside the door. He was. Aaron ran his hand through his own hair, bent down, and began helping Stacey and Kyle.

Stacey tried to focus on page numbers only. It was hard. Her eyes kept scanning the pages. She saw lots of words. She read no sentences; nothing made sense. Like Matt, she wasn't sure if she wanted to know why either.

Kyle pushed himself away from the papers. He couldn't handle it. Already he had read too much.

He wanted an ordered account of why, and he wanted someone else to give it to him. He looked at Aaron, "Will you read it if Matt won't?"

Aaron looked at Kyle and then out the door towards Matt, "Matt'll read it. He just needs some time. I shouldn't have pushed him." He looked back at Kyle, so vulnerable, so scared, so easily swayed. Aaron wondered what kind of effect this was going to have on him. Had Nikki even thought about it, or even cared? Of course she cared, he decided, and looked away from Kyle and back down at the papers that still lay on the floor.

The door opened.

The three, still in the room, looked up. Aaron was the first to look away and continue sorting. He finished after a few seconds, picked the pile up and set it in front of Matt. The others had each taken a place at the table. Aaron took the remaining seat.

Kyle watched Matt expectantly. Aaron watched Kyle watching Matt. Stacey looked down and played with her fingers nervously. Matt glanced at each of them and then read the few words of the first page; the page that had scared Kyle; the page that Aaron had seen, had even known about for so long; the page that Stacey had refused to look at.

"Please understand that, for me, there's only one way out."

Matt looked at the others. Afraid to go on; afraid not to. He shifted to a more comfortable position in the hard wooden chair and turned the page.

"I don't know how each of you is going to respond to this. I hope that by the time I'm finished you'll understand enough to know that it was the only way that I could be happy--at least that's what I believe. I'm sure each of you has had different feelings and responses, remember that as you read this; I, too, have individual feelings and

responses; and just because you may not understand doesn't mean I don't feel the way I do. I have never felt surer of anything in my life. This is the way it has to be-- the only way.

"Remember seven years ago, that party down at Doc's old barn. Man, I can't believe we took Kyle to all those parties; he was only fourteen. Aaron, you weren't around yet; but I told you about it--remember."

Matt paused and looked up at Aaron, who nodded, "I think I know which one she's talking about."

"I d-d-don't know. Th-Th-There were a lot of p-p-parties at Doc's." Matt stared at his little brother. Nikki was right. He had been too young. But he never had any friends of his own; the closest he came to having friends were the ones who teased him about the way he talked.

Matt looked back down at the page, "I'm sure she's going to tell us." He knew which one she was talking about; but Nikki would tell Kyle. This was her ugly baby.

"The date was August 11th, a Saturday night. We got there early, around 7 o'clock, because there wasn't much going on anywhere else. It was hot, remember. I think it must've been 95 degrees, even at that time of night. Anyway, we got into the beer right away. I remember it tasting as muggy as the weather; and that old barn didn't help much; it smelled damp and musty--really stank. We had to drink just to get rid of the smell. Stacey, you brought that guy Tom with you, the one from the photography store; he didn't smell much better than the barn. I remember you keeping your distance; the rest of us did the same--nice guy though; someone should've told him about soap and water, not to mention deodorant.

"Anyway, we started playing caps and everyone got totally wasted. By 9 o'clock, we couldn't smell the barn anymore, but the heat was still bad. Matt, you started talking about your old man--like you always do when you've had too many. Kyle must've been outside taking a leak, because you told us about your dad beating him up. It made me wonder why you never talked about him hitting you; it was always Kyle. Sure you were older and bigger, but he must've hit you when you were Kyle's age. It scared me that you never talked about it. I started thinking about us--you and me--and the possibility of having a family. And I realized that I didn't want a family. I didn't want the responsibility of fucking-up some little kid's mind. And then I started thinking about what I would do with my life if I wasn't going to have a family. There was nothing I wanted to do with it, nothing at all.

"I had another beer. I didn't need it; I wanted it. The night was dull and boring and I started getting depressed.

A few other people joined our group--Mike and Kathy,

Pete, Dave, and I think Sara was there too. Anyway, I

needed some fresh air so I got up and walked out. The air

wasn't that fresh, but at least I escaped the dungeon feeling

I was getting inside the barn. I walked into the corn field--

a beer in my hand--and stumbled through it. Never spilled

my beer; funny how drunks can do that.

"I had just tripped and trampled a couple of corn

stalks when I heard the train horn. I stopped in my tracks,

swaying a little and trying to focus in on the sound. What a

wonderful sound it was. I checked behind me to see if

anyone was there.

It was dark and silent. I could still see the barn and the

lights of the party; I looked back towards the train tracks

again. It was like it had a hold on me. As if someone had

thrown out a lasso, caught me by the neck and was reeling

me in. I ran, trampling corn out of the way. I didn't know

how far the tracks were; I just knew they were there. I

heard the horn again--a long blare followed by two short ones. I figured it was approaching the intersection near Scout's place, and travelling west; it was a freight train--I knew that for sure--because passenger trains didn't use those tracks.

"I rifled the beer bottle into the corn and ran faster. My heart thumping, my mind racing; what was I going to do? That noose kept tugging at my neck and I was trapped. I swear to God it was like being in a trance. I just knew I had to beat the train to the tracks. Sweat soaked by back and forehead, and my chest started to hurt, even so, I needed a cigarette and wondered if I'd have time. All of a sudden I could see the tracks. The whistle blew again. I stopped at the edge of the corn field and lit a cigarette. I couldn't breathe, but I sure as hell could smoke. Man, we're weird creatures.

"I saw the light from the train; it was just getting to the bend. One more road to cross and it would be directly

in front of me. What was I doing? I didn't understand too well back then. The whistle blew--one long, two short--and I stepped onto the tracks. It didn't seem to be moving too fast. Then I heard this voice, 'Hey, what the hell are you doin'. I looked and saw this dark body running along the tracks towards me; it was ahead of the train, but the train was catching up. I started shaking. The body got closer and closer.

I couldn't move. My feet seemed pasted to the tracks. I should've run away from it, down the tracks, outrunning the person, but not the train. Suddenly there was a piercing, screeching noise--I guess the breaks of the train. And this big shape lumbered towards me. The head-light of the train got real close, blinding me, then these arms and a body slapped into me knocking me off the tracks. The kind of thing you only read about in books, right? Or see in the movies? Well, this was real life. I should've gone then. I wouldn't have left so many hurt people behind."

Matt stopped reading. The room was silent.

Kyle could feel a knot tying up in his stomach. A heaviness began moving up his throat. He pushed his chair away from the table, and stood, his hand covering his mouth, and ran from the room.

Silence again.

Matt shook his head, "How the hell could she do this?"

Stacey sighed, resolved to silence.

Aaron's face went hard; pieces could have been chipped out of it. He shoved his chair back, flashed a steely glance in Matt's direction, and walked to a corner. His eyes were damp, as he restrained the tears that Nikki's story had chiseled out of him. He couldn't speak. In his own way, Matt was right; but only in his own way. Unfortunately, Aaron thought, there are too many ways out there.

Stacey bit at her nails, and in a mousy voice asked, "You guys think Kyle's okay?"

Aaron walked towards the door, "I'll go and find him." He left the room.

Stacey looked at Matt, the one person she had ever felt safe with. She despised herself, sometimes, for the way she felt towards him; she didn't know if it was just the brotherly love that she should feel, or not. She studied his features carefully, now.

His face, through the sullenness, had an elegant shape to it--almost beautiful. His colouring was fair, and he had a slight burn on his nose from the day at the beach, yesterday. Just yesterday. Everything had been okay--yesterday. Nikki hadn't been there, of course, but Nikki had been away for nearly five months. Stacey had just been getting used to Nikki's absence. Matt had been showing her a little more attention. Now, she felt guilty.

2

The door opened. Aaron walked in. Kyle slunk in behind him.

"You okay?" Stacey asked.

Kyle nodded; his face was blushed and damp. He sat down.

Matt, ignoring his little brother, stared at Aaron, at the angry eyes, the drawn face. Aaron seemed to understand Nikki better than Matt did, but it didn't mean that Aaron had had loved her more. And he had loved her. Matt knew that. Nikki had told him. Was that another reason for this? He wondered. Matt stared back down at the papers--still quite a few to go.

Aaron sat back down and stared at the others. He rested his forearms on the table and clasped his hands together, settling back in his chair.

"Ready?" Matt asked.

Stacey and Kyle nodded.

Aaron stared at his clasped hands.

"Okay Nikki, what other nightmares do you want to tell us about?" Matt looked down at the page, found his place and continued.

"Ever since that night, suicide has been a shadow over my life. Day in and day out. Every day. Even on good days, something would happen that would make me think of it. Like I hurt someone, or I made the wrong decision, or someone hurt me. I hated myself for thinking about it, and I hated myself for not being able to do anything about it.

Mainly, I just hated myself--for seven years. I guess

something has to come out of feelings like that, eh?

"Why have I hurt so many more people doing this

now instead of seven years ago? Well, I've met a lot of

new people since.

People who I let into my life and then gave a sharp push

out of it. Remember Christina, my friend from work. Man,

we used to talk about everything. She's the one that got me

into reading. Not a day went by I didn't see her with a

book. She knew about all kinds of things--stuff I'd never

even heard of--just from reading novels. And I wanted the

knowledge that she had; the knowledge she had about

people and life. So, I started reading myself. But I was so

far behind. I knew I'd never catch up. You can't start

reading when you're twenty-one and think you're gonna

learn as much as you would have if you'd started reading

when you were twelve. I felt lost; and I got so angry at

myself for wasting so much time, that I almost O.D.'d then. But Matt, you had just brought Aaron into our little group; and he was a new intrigue for me; and I thought I might just want to stick around and figure him out.

"So, I pushed Christina out of my life; I could barely say hi to her when I passed her at work. The only thing she ever did wrong was to make me realize how much time I'd wasted in my life. It wasn't even her fault, but every time I saw her I'd think about it, and then I'd think about death, and I didn't like thinking about that, so I shoved her out of the way and went after something that made me think of life--Aaron. And I left Christina, hurt. I could tell by the look in her eyes when we did speak; she had trusted me, and I let her down.

"Christina wasn't the first or the last person I did that to; she's just an example of all of them. Sometimes I wonder what people ever saw in me in the first place."

Matt stopped, turning the page. He glanced at the others. They were all staring down at their hands. He ran his hand through his hair, took a deep breath, and continued.

"*I'll never forget the first time I met Aaron. I've told Matt about this, but the rest of you don't know.*

"*I got this call from Matt at about 9:30, one Sunday night, he was frantic. A friend of his, from work, had gotten drunk and was hanging from the balcony. It was only three stories, but he would've broken some bones if he'd fallen. I went right over. His friend didn't know I lived down the hall so he didn't expect me to get down there so quickly. He was a-hootin' and a-hollerin' at the top of his lungs. I hung my head over the rail and as soon as he saw me he hoisted* himself *back up onto the balcony, jumped the rail, ran his hand through his hair and said, 'Well, hi there.'*

"Matt was furious, and knocked him out of the way, almost threw him back over the balcony. I laughed, and that didn't help things because the balcony-guy started laughing too.

Matt went back into the apartment, leaving us two hyenas to laugh it out, and got himself a beer. He came back a couple of minutes later, grabbed me and pulled me inside, 'This is my girlfriend,' he stated, stressing the 'my'. Well, that didn't impress me too much. I never was one for being someone else's property. I plainly stated that I belonged to no-one and that I never would and I left.

"But I couldn't move when I got outside the apartment door. My nerves were all tense, my heart was pounding, and I could barely draw a breath. I realized that guy in there had done something to me that Matt had never done-- given me the whirl-berries, as I liked to put it. I finally found enough of myself to move down the hallway, and

once I was moving, I ran. I was scared of the feeling.
Anything new scares me.

"Anyway, that guy, if you haven't already guessed,
was Aaron. I can't believe you let us meet again, Matt.
I mean, you must've known that something might happen.
Didn't you? Guess I'll never know, now."

"No. I guess you never will." Matt wouldn't look
up from the page. He turned it.

"So, did you?" Stacey asked.

Matt looked up, at Stacey, at Kyle, and finally at
Aaron. He looked back at the sheets of paper. "No. I
never suspected a thing," his voice cracked as he spoke.
He stood up, running his fingers through his hair, "Look, I
need a drink." He looked at his watch, "It's 7:30. How
about we go downtown and hit a bar for a couple of beers.
This is pretty heavy stuff. I could sure use a drink." He
glanced at the others, his face flushed.

Aaron was the first to push back his chair, "Sounds great to me." He whacked Kyle gently across the top of his head, "How about you buddy, you thirsty?"

Kyle nodded, "Yeah. Kind of." He got up.

"Stacey?" Matt asked.

She stared down at her hands lying on the table, "Okay." The feet of the chair scratched the floor as she stood. She pushed the chair back in.

Matt picked up the pile of papers, placing the ones he'd already read on the bottom, face up. They all left the room and headed towards the desk, checking in the papers, and confirming that they'd all be back. They were just going for a drink--to clear their heads.

3

Matt decided on 'The Four Seasons', a place where they could grab a beer and a bite if they wanted to. He was hungry. The others agreed, without hesitation. They took a booth near a window at the front of the restaurant--Aaron and Stacey on one side, Matt and Kyle on the other--and stared at the menus.

How anyone could eat right now, Stacey didn't know; but she was sure she couldn't. She stared at the menu; it was what she was supposed to do; but when the waitress came for the order, she would ask for a diet coke only. She had known there was something between Nikki and Aaron; she had been able to tell; but how could she tell Matt without hurting him and making him hate her.

She'd seen it on television how a good friend would speak up to try and save a friend from being hurt and had ended up being hated. And the last thing she wanted, even back then, was for Matt to hate her. So she'd stayed quiet. She might have been wrong anyway. She always stayed quiet; it seemed, to her, the best way to be.

Kyle was numb. He had learned to be that way; his father had taught him. He wouldn't be able to eat anything, but he'd buy some fries to make it look good. He couldn't look at Aaron; he wondered if he'd ever be able to face him again. But he liked Aaron, so there had to be something wrong. It had to be Nikki's fault, he figured, and left it at that. Did it matter anyway, now? Nikki was gone--forever--and Aaron was still here. So is Matt, he thought, and wondered what was going to happen between the two of them. Then he decided to stop thinking about it; it wasn't really his problem, anyway. He was glad his thoughts didn't stutter, and thought about that.

Matt stared at the menu and chewed his nails, a habit he'd picked up as a child in response to his father's beatings; he was glad he didn't stutter. He hadn't noticed the romance signs between Nikki and Aaron because he'd never thought about losing her. She had always been there. It was a fact that she always would be. They'd known each other since kindergarten, had started dating in junior-high, and had held onto each other right through high-school; he never thought it would change. She was his; she always had been. He couldn't imagine her with anyone else. That's how he used to think. How wrong he had been. It was easier to see now; he even felt differently, as if maybe she hadn't been right for him. He closed the menu; he'd have what he always had, a cheeseburger with fries.

Aaron gnawed at the inside of his mouth, his hand behind his neck. He leaned back in the seat and held the menu in front of his face, his neck bent back; it was sore.

They all knew, now, about him and Nikki. That's the way he thought it should've been all along. Nikki never should've kept it quiet. That was half her problem. They were all hurt now. Sure, they'd never be hurt again, by Nikki; but other people were going to pop in and out of their lives making them hell. Aaron knew that was man's destiny, to live in the hell created by everyone else; but he'd conceded to it and would live with it--Nikki couldn't. Ever since he had realized this truth, he knew he would never have kids; he wouldn't knowingly put anyone in hell. He folded the menu and set it on the table; Matt had just put his down. He crossed his arms in front of him, leaned on the table and stared out the window; the sun was starting to go down.

"Are you ready to order?" The voice interrupted all thoughts; it was high pitched and flighty. The four stared at her bleached blonde hair, blue-grey eyes, and then glanced at each other, knowing who would order first.

"I'll have a cheeseburger and fries," Matt said, smiling brightly.

Kyle knew. He'd known it all along. He wondered why it had taken him so long to see it, to acknowledge it; Matt and his dad were identical. Always right; always first; and always the leader. Kyle looked at his brother now, and despised him, and also wondered if he, too, was just like his father. He slid across the seat, bumping Matt out, his hand over his mouth and was gone.

"Shit. Not again. That kid wimps out at the stupidest times."

The waitress had moved closer to the table to let Kyle by, her large, yet figurish, hips very close to Matt's face. He leaned back and smiled at her, his eyes wandering across the matching bumps in her tight nylon uniform.

"Is he okay?"

"Yeah. Don't worry about him. Weak stomach you know. Nothing major."

Stacey almost threw-up herself. She'd never noticed Matt's insensitivity towards his brother before; in fact, she had thought he was great with Kyle. The waitress was looking at her; she could feel those big beautiful, ugly, things staring her down. It was time to talk. "I'll just have a diet coke, please." Stacey didn't look at her; she looked at Matt.

"I'll have a 'Canadian'," Aaron said, peering out the window. He wondered what had upset Kyle; he knew it was more than 'nothing' as Matt had perceived it to be.

"Yeah, I'll take one of those too...and get one for Kyle."

"Three 'Canadians'?" the waitress confirmed in question.

Matt nodded, glancing over at Aaron, who was looking out the window. "Hey bud. No hard feelings, eh? I should've known it was all wrong between Nikki and me. You were her heartthrob; I can live with that."

Aaron looked at Matt. He saw an egotistical bastard and, for the first time since he'd known Matt, he hated every cubical inch of him. He smiled and nodded, "No hard feelings."

"That all?"

Aaron stared at the waitress, then at Matt.

"Yeah Hun., thanks."

The waitress left and Kyle returned to the table. Matt slid out to let him in.

"No, I wanna s-s-sit on the end." Kyle looked at his big brother with intensity.

"Shit Kyle, when're you gonna grow up?" Matt repeated words he had heard his father speak. He almost stammered, but realized how, for once, his father was right.

"Knock it off Matt. Leave the kid alone." Aaron controlled his temper, he didn't want Matt to know how angry he really was.

"Kid?" Matt's voice rose, and he looked around him, continuing in a lower tone, "He's twenty-one for Christ's sake. It's about time he started acting it." He glared at Aaron and stared out the window.

Aaron decided that it was best to let it drop. Matt, being tyrannically right, wouldn't let it drop without having the final word, and Aaron was sure that Kyle didn't need any more ridicule than he had already had. "You okay Kyle?" Aaron asked, examining Kyle's face. He looked like a little kid. He'd always been treated like a little kid; how could he be expected to grow up. Realizing this, Aaron secretly vowed never to treat him like a little kid again.

Kyle nodded. He knew that they all thought he was a sissy. They only had him around because he was Matt's little brother. After today, he decided, he would find his own friends.

He wouldn't want to hang around his father, anyway, and now that Matt was just like his father, Kyle couldn't stand the thought of being around him.

The waitress came back with the drinks and a napkin, knife, and fork, for Matt. She smiled suggestively at Matt, who, this time, didn't respond. The smile disappeared and she left.

They each took a sip of their drinks.

Kyle knew Matt had ordered the beer for him. It was too strong. He had always thought regular beer was too strong, but he dare not say anything or they'd all laugh. He couldn't look at any of them; he could feel how hot his face was. They could all tell how weak he was. He knew they could; they didn't know he knew, but he knew--now. Then he realized how many 'n's he'd thought without stuttering, and he thought about that.

Aaron ran his fingers up and down the beer bottle, glancing at Kyle every once in a while. He wanted to get him alone, away from the other two and talk to him. It was Kyle he was most concerned about right now. And all sorts of images flew through his mind as he tried to figure out how all of this was going to affect him. Maybe Nikki hadn't thought about it well enough; and he started to get angry at her. His fingers picked at the beer label; it ripped. He pulled a cigarette out of his package and held it out for Kyle, who caught Aaron's eye for a second, and took the smoke. Aaron took one out for himself and put the pack away.

They lit their cigarettes. The blue smoke hanging over the table. Matt's food came. The waitress set it down through the smoke. Aaron and Kyle looked at each other. Aaron smiled. Kyle pulled his eyes away.

During this time Stacey had been sipping her diet coke. It was almost gone. She wouldn't ask for another one. Nobody seemed to have noticed that she was still there and she didn't want to draw attention to this fact. She'd seen Aaron watching Kyle a couple of times and figured he wanted to talk to him alone. She understood why; he didn't want Matt's two cents worth corrupting the poor kid. Most of the time she had been watching Matt; trying to figure him out. He seemed to have changed all of a sudden. She no longer liked him and this bothered her because she knew she really did like him. Then she wondered if maybe she'd seen him unclearly before, blinded, as they say, by the feelings she had for him. But she wondered why those feelings had left. Then she knew: Nikki had taken them with her, had changed all the feelings in all of them. She thought about this as she drained the last of her diet coke, and played quietly with the straw.

Matt picked at his food. He wasn't hungry, he supposed, because Kyle's throwing up had made him queasy. That his father could be right about something, even something as obvious as this, bothered him. Aaron was babying Kyle; he didn't want him to grow up. Kyle needed to grow up; Matt knew this, but he wasn't sure how to go about doing it. It was his responsibility, of course; his father wasn't about to do anything about it, and neither was Aaron--obviously. He knew it was on his plate, again, to take care of his little brother. Just as he had always had to do. Well, he'd practically raised him, taking him everywhere, showing him things, teaching him about life, and now he had to get him to grow up. He wondered if it would ever stop, and figured it would be his responsibility until the day one of them died. And then he thought about Nikki; she had made everything stop. But she hadn't had any responsibilities; this he knew for sure, because she had complained about it often enough. He would never understand why Nikki had killed herself, never in a thousand years. He put his hamburger down--half eaten-- and threw a napkin over it. He gulped back most of his remaining beer, looked at the drinks on the table, and quietly belched.

"You guys ready to go, or ya want another drink?" Matt asked, not looking at anyone in particular.

"I'm done," Aaron said, matter-of-factly.

"Me too," Stacey spoke.

Kyle shrugged his shoulders. He wanted another beer--a light one he could actually enjoy. That's what he wanted, what he did was reach into his pocket for some money.

"I got it." Matt said impatiently as he waited for his little brother to move.

Kyle looked at him. He was sad that Matt wasn't who he had thought he was. He slid out of the seat and let Matt pass, watching him approach the cash register.

"Your bill," their waitress hustled after Matt, her boobs bouncing.

The three still at the table watched the spectacle quietly. Aaron shook his head, clipped Kyle playfully across the ear, and put a friendly arm around Stacey, "Let's follow our master," he said, and obeyed his own command.

4

Matt lead them through the corridors, got the pile of papers, and went into the small interrogation room. They had already spent two hours in there, Matt wondered how many more there would be. He shook the papers in his hand and felt guilty about being glad that Nikki was gone. Right now he wished he were gone too. But that was foolish, he knew, because things like this didn't change anything anyway. He took the same chair he had sat on the last time they had been in here, turned it around and sat on it backwards, his legs straddling the back; he pulled his fingers through his hair and looked at the others, his face serious.

The others also took their previous places; it seemed the thing to do. Stacey always took the same seat she'd had before, no matter where she was--home, school, or visiting; she liked to be familiar with where she sat. Aaron took the same seat because he wanted to be able to see all of them without turning his head too much. The table was a hard-wood rectangle; Aaron sat at the short end, opposite Matt. Kyle took the same seat because it was the only one left by the time he sat down; actually, he didn't want to sit down at all. None of them turned their chairs around.

Matt watched them follow his lead and wondered how he had so much power over them; a part of him liked it; a part of him didn't. He leaned over the back of his chair and found his spot in the text.

"*Anyway, Aaron and I started seeing each other. Neither of us ever felt really comfortable because both of us liked Matt a lot.*

But we couldn't stay away from each other. We never did anything--sexually, I mean--at first; we'd just go out and talk, or play pool, real innocent things. We liked each other's company and it seemed the thing to do. We did this for four years.

"I think we fell in love. Aaron would never admit the word existed. I merely question its meaning; I mean, what is love but what you think it is. We knew we were going to have to tell Matt because we really wanted to sleep with each other. I was still sleeping with Matt; although, not very often. I'm sure you can remember when I used to get all those headaches, Matt. I felt too guilty to sleep with you, and I was too scared to tell you. Then you gave me the ring."

Matt stopped reading but stared at the page, "I thought she wanted it; I thought that was why she was holding out on me, because she wanted a ring."

Aaron looked at him; he felt strangely sorry for Matt, seeing Matt's perspective in a little better light. Before, Matt had seemed arrogant, now, he seemed lost. Aaron realized that Matt had never thought about the possibility of losing Nikki.

"Had she asked you for a ring?" Stacey wiped a tear from her eye; she, too, was feeling for Matt.

Matt still didn't look up, "No. She was too nice to do that. At least that's what I thought."

Kyle was brewing in anger. He clenched his teeth and stood up. Standing up was what he wanted to do anyway; why shouldn't he? Kyle saw Matt as insensitive and cruel; he should have asked her what was wrong before he jumped to his ever-right conclusion; a mirror-image of his father; like father, like son--like sons?

Kyle held on to his stomach; he didn't want to get sick again; they would all laugh and know he was a weakling. He tried to stop it.

He didn't figure he had much else to throw-up. He ran out the door.

Aaron went out after him. He wanted to find out what was really wrong. He didn't know if it was his right or if Kyle would even talk to him, but he felt he had to try.

Stacey pulled her chair closer to Matt and rested her hand on his arm. She looked at him and smiled; he smiled, briefly, in return. She peered into his green eyes and saw what she had once seen before--pain, anger, and fear.

"Did you love her?" she asked.

He shrugged his shoulders. "I never remembered life without her. That's all. We were just together. All the time. I never thought it would change."

"So, you never really loved her?"

He shrugged again and felt his own stomach turning queasy, "I don't know."

Stacey leaned back in the chair, taking her hand off of Matt's arm. She was drawn to him again. The feelings she'd had towards him in the restaurant were gone. She wondered where they'd gone to and if they would return. She loved Matt; she knew that now; and, she didn't feel guilty.

Matt felt his insides churning as he thought about all the wasted years. He wondered why he hadn't felt this way before, when he'd first learned about Aaron and Nikki. He'd believed that it wouldn't last. It hadn't mattered what they had told him, Nikki was his. Life couldn't be any other way.

He let them think it was okay; but, secretly, he thought it wouldn't last. He thought Nikki would come running back to him; that she'd get sick of Aaron's philosophy of life, and want to return to Matt's stable realities.

He had been wrong, and that's what had killed Nikki, he thought now; she had known he would never let go. He controlled the tremour in his lip and the queasy feeling in his stomach, as he had learned to do.

Kyle walked into the room, followed by Aaron, who sat down. Kyle stood in the corner farthest away from Matt; he stared at the floor.

Matt looked at his little brother and wanted to cry. He knew he would not. Kyle still had to grow up and Matt knew that controlling things was all a part of it. Kyle would never see him cry, just as neither of them had ever seen their father cry. Learning not to cry, and not to get sick, were at least two things Matt would have to teach Kyle about growing up. He looked down at the page. He wanted to finish reading and get out of there.

Matt read on, "*A ring, Matt. My first thought was what in God's name would you go and do that for; had I ever asked for one? Then I realized that we'd been together for so long that, really, it wasn't such a stupid idea on your part after all. I guess you can see how this confused me so much. And I hate to hurt you the way that I just have, but it had to be done or I would have hurt you for the rest of your life. I didn't have the heart to tell you I couldn't accept the ring. Through all of this, Aaron stood by me and let me make the decisions that I felt I had to make. But we were so unhappy, trying to hide it, knowing it must have shown.*

"*We held things together for a couple of weeks after you'd given me the ring. But we began to get more and more attracted to each other, probably because it was something I was denying us of doing. Then one day we went to the beach together.*

The rest of you were all busy or else just didn't want to go, I can't exactly remember. Anyway, we went by ourselves.

"That night, on the beach, Aaron made love to me like I've never had it before. It was so real, so meaningful, so full of love. I know this hurts, Matt, and I'm sorry, but I have to let you know how deep the feelings were that lead to my final decision."

Matt stopped reading.

Silence.

Kyle stood, stone faced, in the corner and looked at his brother. He thought that Matt deserved to be told. Maybe facing this thing with Nikki would make Matt look more closely at himself and see what he had become. Kyle no longer cared how his brother felt because he didn't think his brother had any feelings.

Stacey took a deep breath, looked at Aaron and Kyle, and then down at the papers. She didn't think either Aaron or Kyle was going to rescue Matt. "You want me to read for a while," she asked, and reached for the papers.

Matt pulled them away from her. "No. I'll do it."

Stacey knew he was trying to act strong, and at one time she might have thought that he was heartless; but, now, she just felt sorry for him, because she knew he was denying himself the right to feel sad and hurt. Stacey watched as he took the papers back. She wanted to tell him it was okay to feel the way he really did, that none of them were going to criticize his real feelings, but she could not. He would only get angry. She might try it sometime when Aaron and Kyle weren't there. She thought she could break him if they were alone.

"Matt, what you and I had was wonderful. But it wasn't ecstasy. Sex was just one of those things--highly overrated. And I didn't really care if we did it or not. You, of course, wanted it all the time--most men do, I've heard."

Matt stopped and cleared his voice. He was getting angry with Nikki for discussing their sex-life like this. He wanted to skip over all this stuff. But he knew the others would be able to tell; and he had to show Kyle that he was strong, that he could handle anything. He was being a role model, and wouldn't let himself forget it.

He continued. *"I care for you very deeply, Matt. We had been together for so long that we never stopped to think about whether it was right or not. We just lived. I loved Aaron; and sex with someone you love is almost indescribable; I really hope you'll all experience it one day--and protect it."*

Matt stopped again. He looked at Aaron who was staring right back at him. Matt swallowed hard, trying to fight the nauseous feeling as it rose up his throat, "So, you have quite the dick, do you?" he smiled.

Aaron held Matt's eyes with his. There were a thousand things that he wanted to say. He fought with his mind, trying to make sense out of chaos, and holding Matt's eyes. He didn't know whether he should break Matt down and reveal all the hidden fears and tears, or if he should allow Matt to appear cold, confirming Kyle's ogre view of him. Aaron thought that to be real was the most important thing in life; and that, if you weren't real, then you weren't really living. But he didn't want to be judgmental. And what if he was wrong?

Matt pulled his eyes away from Aaron's, looked at his little brother and winked, "Better get your sex-ed from Aaron here. He seems to know how to make the girls scream." He looked back at Aaron, smiling.

Aaron refused to join in Matt's little game and decided just to ignore it and hope it went away. He didn't stop looking Matt straight in the eye; he wasn't afraid of him; he just didn't know the best way to deal with Matt's true emotions--if he had them; and Aaron believed that he did.

"Anyway," Matt said, "We were here to discuss Nikki's suicide, not her sexual affairs. She certainly has had some phenomenal experiences in her short twenty-five years. I kinda think she missed out though; she never got married or had kids. How can life be complete without them? I would've let go of her eventually. She could of had you and her ecstasy. You sure you were that good, Aaron? Why'd she leave you?"

Aaron, still unnerved, looked straight at Matt, "If you keep reading, maybe we'll find out. Don't worry, Matt. I'm gonna get my chance to be hurt, too."

Matt flinched at the word `hurt'; he didn't think he was acting like he was hurt and wondered where Aaron had got the idea from.

5

Matt looked back down at the papers and continued reading.

"Matt, if you haven't realized it yet, I hope you will in time, that you never loved me as a lover. We were more like old friends than anything else. It wasn't Aaron's fault, it wasn't mine, and it wasn't yours; it was life, fate, maybe. I hope the rest of you can understand, too. And don't give in to anything less than real love because you'll only end up getting hurt.

"I don't have anything else to say about my relationships with Aaron or Matt. I only hope that everyone will understand how difficult it all was for me."

"And that's why she killed herself?" Kyle interrupted.

Matt looked at his little brother and held the remaining pages up for him to see, "Must be more than that, Kyle, we've got a few pages left to go."

"Oh." Kyle said and stared down at his shoes.

Nobody noticed that Kyle hadn't stuttered his question. Not even Kyle, himself.

Matt read on. *"The next problem came a couple of months after Aaron and I had been at the beach. I'd missed my period. I kept hoping it was anxiety over my relationships, but I finally went to the doctor and had the pregnancy test. It was positive.*

I couldn't tell anyone, because everything was such a big secret. I didn't know how Aaron was going to respond; although, I was sure he would want me to get an abortion-- which is something I could never do. He would never have kids; and I would never have an abortion."

"Holy shit," Matt interrupted himself, "that's why she went away. She had the fuck'n kid."

Aaron stood up and paced the room. How could she do this to him? Was she sure it was his kid; of course he knew it had to have been, but he couldn't shake the thought that it was Matt's.

Kyle slid his back down the wall, his knees drawn to his chest, his head in his hands.

Stacey stared at the wall. At a small dot, maybe it was a hole from a picture that had once hung there. She couldn't believe all this. It was like 'The Young and The Restless' to her; it had to be make-believe.

"She left a fuck'n kid without a mother. Nikki, I had you pegged all wrong," Matt was saying. "Where on earth did I get the idea you were sensitive and caring. God, was I wrong about you."

Kyle looked up at his brother. He spoke softly. "Give her a chance, Matt. You always jump to conclusions about things without giving people a chance to explain themselves," he turned his head away and mumbled, "just like the old man."

"Just like what?" Matt yelled and rose from his chair.

Aaron moved to protect Kyle; but didn't need to because Kyle was already standing and prepared to fight. Aaron backed away, remembering the promise he'd made to himself in the restaurant.

"The old man, Matt," Kyle snapped back, and took a step towards him. He was, after all, bigger than Matt, why should he be frightened of him. "You're sounding more and more like him every day. I realized it today at the restaurant and I've been able to see it ever since. You give a shit about one person, and one person only-- yourself. You're a selfish bastard, and you're just like him." Kyle stopped, realizing he hadn't stuttered. This gave him more confidence as he stared his brother down.

Matt looked as if he was going to say something, but, instead, he pushed his chair out of the way and left the room. This time the others couldn't see his shadow on the other side of the door.

Aaron, too, had noticed that Kyle hadn't stuttered and he felt a certain pride for him, thinking the kid was going to be okay.

Aaron sat back down, head in hands, and thought about his own kid, that he'd just found out about. All those things he'd let Nikki know, about not wanting to bring kids into this world. He felt sick. He wanted to read on. He didn't want to wait for Matt. Sweat formed on his forehead; he wiped at it. Kyle came and sat beside him. Aaron looked at him and smiled, weakly.

"You gonna be okay?" Kyle asked.

Aaron shook his head and ran his fingers back and forth across the table, "Your guess is as good as mine." But he smiled; Kyle had come a long way in a few short hours; Aaron was proud of him, and so he smiled.

"I'm gonna go check on Matt," Stacey walked towards the door, "This has all gotta be pretty hard on him." She left the room.

Aaron nodded and looked at Kyle. "Yeah. It's gotta be."

Kyle stood up, angry again. "He deserved it."

"Nobody deserves something like this."

Kyle looked at Aaron carefully, as if trying to understand what Aaron was saying, when he already had it all figured out. It was all Matt's fault as far as Kyle was concerned; how could it be hard on him? Matt, being just like his father, as Kyle was now convinced he was, deserved to have everyone close to him die; then, maybe he would appreciate what he had. Kyle sighed and sat on the floor in a corner behind Aaron.

Aaron turned on his chair to face him. "Matt is hurting, Kyle. It's just a matter of time before it all comes out. He's hiding everything because he wants you, and Stacey and I, to think he's indestructible. Unfortunately, all you see is your father. Maybe the two of you could learn something about your father from all this." He went on, as if talking to himself, "People are so damned judgmental. If it's not their way, then it's not the right way.

There are thousands of right ways; everybody has their own."

Kyle was silent, as if taking all this in, "Like Nikki?" He asked, after several minutes.

Aaron looked at Kyle and smiled, "Yeah, just like Nikki." And he knew he would have to remember this as he listened to the rest of Nikki's story. And he thought about the child, knowing it was his, and knowing he would never see it; he would never want to.

The door opened and Stacey came back in. "Matt's gonna be a minute. He went to get us all a pop." She looked at Kyle and spoke softly, "He's hurting, even if it doesn't show," and she sat down.

Kyle watched her. Her red hair standing straight up on top, cropped short at the sides, the back long and thinned out.

She had just repeated what Aaron had told him and he sat and let it soak in. He realized he had a lot to learn about people and life. He wasn't sure he was going to like all the puzzles involved, and wondered why people couldn't just be who they were, instead of pretending all the time. He sighed again and rested his head back against the wall.

Matt walked in with four pops clutched between his stomach and his hands. He handed the diet coke to Stacey; the rest were all cokes; he gave one to Aaron and one to Kyle, and sat down with his, popping it open.

"We'd better keep at this," Matt said, "or we're gonna be here all night." He found his place on the page and continued reading.

"But, that's not the only reason that I couldn't tell you, Aaron. I didn't want to tie you down to anything, either. You're a free-spirit.

I always admired that about you. You probably would've let me keep the baby, and married me; but you never would've been happy, and I couldn't do that to you.

"And not only that, I wasn't sure I wanted the responsibility of raising a child. I wasn't ready, myself, for children. So that's why I had to leave. All around, it was better for everyone; no more curve balls into our relationships; no more decisions, that none of us needed, or wanted. I would go away, give the baby up and come back, facing whatever might have transpired while I was gone."

Matt stopped reading; he could feel the lump forming in his throat. He looked at Kyle and his damp eyes, and realized that Kyle, too, was trying not to cry. Matt cleared his throat.

"She still hadn't decided to kill herself, yet. She'd solved all the problems so that none of us would have to deal with them." Stacey broke down.

Matt got up and walked over to her; he knelt down and held her. She sobbed into his shirt.

Kyle watched as his brother held Stacey; he still wasn't sure what was real and what wasn't. Then he saw the tear squeeze out of Matt's eye. Kyle looked away; he didn't want to see his brother cry.

Aaron stared at his fingers that were running back and forth across the table; he had known that Nikki was suicidal; she had told him. But he had also thought, as she had told him, that he had taken some of those feelings away. When she left, five months ago, he reconsidered the idea, and came to the conclusion that he wasn't enough to stop her from doing what she would ultimately do, and he had come to terms with the fact that when she returned, she would be dead. Her death wasn't a shock to him; the fact that she had planned on coming back, was. That, and the child.

Stacey pulled herself gently away from Matt, and he leaned back; they looked each other's eyes; Matt pulled his away first and stood up.

"You gonna be okay?" Matt asked her.

She nodded, wiping away a few remaining tears.

Kyle took a sip of his pop. He'd forgotten he had it. He was still sitting on the floor in the corner.

Aaron watched his fingers, still confused.

Matt sat back down and picked up the papers. He knocked them against the table to square the edges, not knowing why he was doing it, but doing it all the same. He looked at Aaron and wondered what was going through his mind at that moment. It was his child--Aaron's--and Matt knew it; he and Nikki hadn't slept together since she and Aaron had.

And now Aaron had to deal with the fact that there was a kid out there without a mother or a father, and Matt wondered how Aaron would respond.

So far, he'd seemed copasetic with it all; although, Matt thought he sensed some confusion in those big brown eyes.

Aaron looked at Matt and wondered if it was a judgmental or a questioning eye he had just caught. He decided he didn't really care. Matt would have to learn his own lessons, as Aaron was busy learning his.

6

Matt read. *"Where I am right now is not important. The people are great and they're treating me well. They have agreed to take care of everything for the baby and I trust them. This is all going to sound kind of funny; me talking in the present, you being in the future, and all of us dealing with the past.*

"The baby is due in one month. I started writing all this down yesterday, which is when I finally made my decision not to return at all. I suppose the thought had crossed my mind before I even left, but Aaron had crossed it out, and I really believed that I'd be able to return. Things didn't go exactly as I'd expected they would-- obviously.

"I kept my part-time job at the shoe store; I got a transfer to the store out here. I wanted to be able to pay my way as much as possible; although Pat and Irene have been great and didn't want much. I did, of course, have to buy a couple of track suits and a new bra as the pregnancy progressed. And I don't make that much money, so what I've been giving them is very little.

"I just took a leave of absence from L.S., so I could've got my full-time job back. Maybe I shouldn't have kept the job at the shoe store, because that was where I did all the thinking that I probably shouldn't have done.

"What I thought about was the big secret I was going to have to keep from you guys, and I didn't know if I was going to be able to do it. I'm terrible with secrets, and it would have haunted me forever.

Yesterday, I decided that you guys had been used to life without me for four months, and it wouldn't take long for you to get used to me being gone forever. And I've settled into this conclusion quite nicely, and feel really satisfied with it. Maybe I'm being selfish; but, then again, maybe it's about time I was. The only reason I haven't done this until now is because I was thinking of you guys, and, I guess to be honest, the idea that something good might just come out of my life.

"Well, I can't make myself feel that way anymore. Too many years of false hope have gone by for me to believe in dreams anymore. I just want to let it all go. I don't want to go back to L.S., dragging my ass around, hating every minute I'm there.

Why can't I do something else? Because it would end up being exactly the same. I mean, I thought I'd like E.C.E., and I didn't; then there was Social Work, and that was another joke; the next thing I try will be the same; at least the benefits and money were good at L.S..

"Anyway, being away from you guys made me realize that I wasn't living for anything worthwhile, and I just got sick of not wanting to be anywhere. I don't want to be here; I don't want to be there; but there isn't really anywhere that I do want to be. My only worry right now is that the baby will be affected in some way by all of this. You know, all that pre-natal trauma they talk about these days. I just hope that I've been calm enough through all of this, not to have left a mark on him--or her, I guess."

Matt paused, taking a large swallow from his coke.

"You know where she was, don't you." Stacey said to Matt.

Matt looked at Aaron, who looked at Matt. They stared at each other for several seconds. Matt pulled his eyes away and looked at Stacey. He rubbed his eyes, as if he were just waking up, and shrugged his shoulders, "Don't know for sure."

Kyle stood up and paced the far wall. His bum and legs were sore from sitting on the floor; he rubbed them, and stretched, and sat down at the table, opposite Stacey. He wondered why it mattered, now, anyway; there was nothing they could do. Kyle chewed at his nails and wondered what it was he was missing in the stares that were being thrown around the room.

Aaron got up and walked to the wall that Kyle had just left; he leaned back against it, "I need a smoke," he said, and left the room.

Kyle looked at Matt, waiting for him to say something. When it was obvious that Matt wasn't about to say anything, Kyle got up and left the room. He didn't say anything, figuring if no-one was going to talk to him, he wasn't going to talk to anyone either. But he was confused, and couldn't understand what the big deal was about where Nikki had been.

"She put those names in there for a reason, Matt. She knows we know who they are and where they live. She wants us to see the kid."

Matt looked at Stacey and rubbed his chin; he could feel the roughness of hair starting to come in, "I need to go home for a shit, shower, and shave."

"Matt." Stacey nearly yelled, which was really out of her character.

Matt looked at her blue eyes; he sensed the anger, and the hope. He knew she was the motherly type, but he didn't know what she was going to get out of seeing the kid.

"Look Stacey, Nikki has planned this down to a 'T'. The kid will be long-gone. Besides, what good would it do? What's the point?"

Matt watched the disappointment cloud over Stacey's eyes. He wasn't trying to be insensitive, but he knew that's what it looked like. He didn't know what to say, so he let her think whatever it was she wanted to about him. He didn't think it much mattered anyway. He took another sip of his pop.

Stacey knew Nikki had told them the names for a reason. Nikki was always doing things like that. 'Read between the lines' she used to say. And that's how they'd always had to figure Nikki out, until now--between the lines.

Matt was being unresponsive, but Stacey was sure he felt it too. Then again, she thought, it isn't his kid. And she wondered if maybe he was right; it was Aaron's kid; if Aaron wanted to see it, then Aaron could choose. Stacey felt empty; she wanted to see the child because he or she was a part of Nikki, not because there was a father at all. She sighed and leaned back in the chair, waiting for Kyle and Aaron to return.

Matt flipped through the remaining pages; there were only a few left; he was glad, because he was getting tired and needed another beer.

Kyle followed several steps behind Aaron, through the halls, across the highly polished floor of the main entrance, and out the front doors. Aaron had a cigarette out of the pack and lit it as he went through the doors.

Kyle fumbled for his own cigarettes in his shirt pocket, but not before Aaron was holding one out for him. Kyle took it, saying thanks.

They stood silently. Aaron hoisted himself up onto the concrete wall that lined the ramp down to the sidewalk. Kyle stood, his back against the wall, beside Aaron. It was dark, but flood-lights lit the area around them.

Aaron stared up at the sky, watching the soft clouds shimmer past the moon, creating a fantastic picture. He stared up like this for some time.

Kyle stared down at his feet, blowing smoke rings. He looked up at Aaron once or twice, about to say something, but looked back down at his shoes again. He wasn't sure what it was he wanted to say; although, he thought they should be saying something.

"What do you think, kiddo?" Aaron finally broke the silence.

Kyle looked up at him. "I don't know."

Aaron smiled and mussed Kyle's hair. "Come on. You gotta have something to say about all of this."

Kyle shrugged and looked back down at his shoes, which, he noticed now, needed replacing; the right toe was all torn out, and the left one had a ripped instep seam; he scuffed them against the ground.

"What do you think about it?" Kyle asked Aaron.

"I knew." He said.

Kyle stepped away from the wall and faced Aaron, "You knew? Why the hell didn't you do something about it?"

"She didn't want me to."

Kyle thought about it for a minute. "How do you know she didn't want you to."

"If she'd wanted someone to do something about it she would've told Matt, or Stacey, maybe even you--I don't know; but, she told me because she knew I wouldn't do anything about it."

Aaron looked up at the sky again, "We'd talked about stuff like this before; she knew I'd never interfere as long as the decision was rational."

"You think suicide is rational?" Kyle asked, genuinely interested.

Aaron looked at Kyle, nodding his head, "Yeah, I think it can be. I mean people get married and pregnant-- not even in that order--and everybody thinks those are rational decisions, right?"

"Aaron, that's different. You're not even making sense."

"I'm not? What happened to your folks?"

Kyle went and stood back against the wall; he was blushing and wanted to get out of the light. What his parents had done was a nightmare to him; he hated to even think about it. "That's d-d-different, too," he stuttered, realizing the fault immediately.

Aaron, noticing the stutter, kept silent. He didn't want to push Kyle too far, and decided that maybe he wasn't ready to understand.

Kyle had finished the cigarette and lit up another, offering one to Aaron, who took it.

"I-I know what your s-s-saying," Kyle said and hung his head, "I've even thought about it once or twice."

Aaron studied him. Kyle's long blonde hair shadowed his face and fell over his bright blue eyes, which Aaron couldn't see from his position. "If you ever think about it again, come and talk to me first," Aaron said, "It has to be the right decision."

Kyle nodded his head, still looking down.

"Promise?"

He nodded his head.

Aaron looked up, again. The clouds were getting wispier, making the moon look haunting, as if werewolves should be out that night.

"So, what about the baby? You know about that too?" Kyle asked.

"No. That, I didn't know about."

"Are you mad?"

"No. She made the right decision."

"But, it was your kid too. Don't you even want to know what happened to it?"

"Nikki took care of it. I trust her."

"But you're the kid's father."

"I'll never be anyone's father," Aaron said and jumped down from the wall.

"You'd make a good father," Kyle said softly.

Aaron barely heard him, and he pretended that he hadn't, "Come on. The others are waiting, and probably getting mad."

They walked silently back to the room.

7

Matt was pacing the room when Aaron and Kyle returned, he looked up and forced a smile. He had thought about going out to get them, but decided against it; he wasn't sure if he wanted to accidentally hear what they were talking about. He was angry because this was taking so long, and just wanted to get it over and done with, so he could get on with his own life, which had taken a sudden turn that he was going to have to slow down for. He was not impressed by that thought, and felt himself getting angry with Nikki again.

"Nice of you to show up," Matt said.

Aaron thought of apologizing, but abandoned it; he had needed the time, and refused to excuse himself for something that he knew he needed. "No problem." He said and sat down.

Kyle, afraid to speak since the return of the stutter, said nothing and sat down in his chair. That the stuttering had left and returned by its own power frightened him. He wondered if he would ever have the courage to speak again. It had felt so good not to stutter; he had had a taste of it; it would be much harder to talk, now. He sat, head hanging, chewing the inside of his mouth, and wondered what Nikki was going to tell them next. Despite his conversation with Aaron, he still thought that Nikki had been wrong, and that something else could have been done. Although, he didn't know what.

Stacey was getting tired, and for a couple of minutes had been trying to figure out what day it was, her mind being so jumbled with other thoughts and concerns, that she couldn't honestly remember if she would have to get up for work the next morning, or not. Nikki had been out of their lives for so long that, as Nikki had said, it wouldn't be that difficult to come to terms with all of this-- except for the baby. Stacey had a problem with the baby-- she wanted to see it. She glanced at Aaron, wondering how he felt about all of this.

Matt started reading, *"Anyway, that's about all I have to say. I love all of you. A love that goes out in four completely different ways. I never wanted to hurt anyone; I won't anymore; I feel good, and relieved for the first time in my life. Maybe you can understand that, maybe you can't. Take care. Love, Nikki."*

Matt held up the remaining pages, "I guess she thought of something else. It doesn't end here, guys."

He continued reading, *"Sorry about this; but I've been doing a little more thinking--dangerous thing. I had the baby two days ago; it was a boy. He's beautiful. He almost made me change my mind; but only for selfish reasons. His best life is here. I can't give him the things he deserves, and he deserves the best.*

"I've been concerned, though, that I haven't been fair to Aaron. You had no say in any of this, and he's your child. I know how you feel about kids and that's why I never gave this a second thought; but, that was before I saw that wonderful little bundle. You have the right to see him, Aaron, if you've changed your mind about anything. Pat and Irene have agreed to let you see him if that's what you want. I told them you wouldn't want to keep him--that, I'm pretty sure of--although, you probably would make a terrific father. Matt and Stacey both know where I am, now. All you have to do is call."

Matt looked at Aaron and back down at the page; he looked at Stacey, seeing the shine in her eyes, the smile hidden behind her frown; she had been right. He had a problem with other people being right, especially if it made him wrong.

"They live--"

"I don't want to know." Aaron interrupted.

Matt looked at him.

"Aaron, are you sure?" Stacey asked, straightening up, genuinely perplexed by his statement.

"I'm sure. Look, get on with the note, will you. Everybody's tired; it's been a long day. There can't be much left now. Let's just finish it, so we can carry on with our own lives."

Matt smiled smugly to himself. He knew that he and Aaron were similar in some ways; and getting this over and done with was one way. He settled back in his chair, *"We call--"*

"Wait Matt." Stacey persisted, "Aaron, I think you need to do more thinking about this. I know you're not insensitive to kids, I've seen you with them; you're great with them, actually. What's the problem here? This is your own flesh and blood we're talking about. You've gotta have some sort of bond with this kid, don't you?"

Aaron stood up, pacing the far wall.

"God, please don't go out for another smoke." Matt said, exasperated.

"Matt, shut-up." Stacey surprised herself, but knew that when she thought something should be a certain way, she would go to any lengths to get it done; and she believed that Aaron needed to do more thinking about this. The child had surfaced new emotions in her, and she believed that children belonged with their natural parents, whoever that may be. She also strongly believed that Aaron would make a good parent.

"Stacey, forget it. I'm not interested in the kid, okay? The kid is better off without me."

"How can you say that?"

"Because I know I'd make a shitty father."

"But, you--"

"Stacey." His voice was stern, but he didn't yell; he knew he could keep calm, it really didn't mean that much to him, anyway.

The room fell silent.

Stacey slouched into the chair, obviously trying to think of some way to convince Aaron that he was wrong.

Aaron remained standing. "Finish reading, Matt. Let's get this over and done with."

Matt continued. *"We called him 'Troy'. I've always loved that name. I guess in some ways I'm sorry I'm going to miss his growing up, his dreams, his life.*

But all I have to do is remind myself of how I'd fuck him up, and it all goes away. This is it guys; my final day; what a fucking relief. Good-bye."

Matt sighed, straightening the papers to return them to the clerk. He sensed Aaron's movement back to the table and watched him sit down. Matt was determined not to stay in this room any longer than he had to, and he hoped that Aaron didn't want to stay and talk. Another beer was what Matt needed. They could talk at his place, over a beer if they wanted to. He stood up, the papers in his hand.

"I'm going home. You guys can come over if you want. I just need to get out of this room; it's taken us three hours to get through twelve pages of bullshit, and I need a beer. I'll meet you at my place, if you're coming." Matt left the room.

Aaron stared at the fingers he was running back and forth across the table. Stacey stared at Aaron. Kyle watched his brother disappear down the hall, and then watched Aaron watch his fingers.

Aaron felt their judgmental eyes upon him and he wanted to scream; but he, too, was judging himself. He still wanted to scream, and if he had really felt free to do whatever he pleased, that is exactly what he would have done. Instead, he watched his fingers, and felt that, for some reason, those judgmental eyes were right; he thought that he should, at least, care about this kid, that was his. But so much of him didn't want to care, and that the little bit of him that did was drowned out. He looked at the two pair of eyes that seemed to be judging, and he smiled.

"Okay," he said, "I'll at least think about it."

Kyle and Stacey both smiled back.

"Come on. Let's get out of here before they lock us in." Aaron stood up, heading for the door.

"You going to Matt's?" Stacey asked.

Aaron looked from Stacey to Kyle, "Not right now. Maybe later," and he walked out the door.

"Are you going?" She asked Kyle as they were walking down the hall.

Kyle shook his head. He wanted to stay with Aaron, if Aaron would let him.

They got outside into the cool night. A strong breeze had come up since Aaron and Kyle had last been out, and it looked as if a storm might drop in. Aaron and Kyle both lit cigarettes. Stacey walked down the ramp with them, but turned the opposite way at the bottom.

"I'm going over to Matt's. I'll see you guys there if you come."

"Bye Stacey."

Kyle raised his hand in a half-wave and turned to follow Aaron. They walked several blocks before Kyle realized where Aaron was going, and wondered if he wanted to be alone. But Kyle didn't want to be alone, and he didn't want to go to Matt's, so he followed silently, hoping that if he was quiet enough it would be okay for him to be there. He felt slightly awkward, as if he were invading a space that wasn't his to invade. He dropped back, several feet behind Aaron, staring at his feet, but making sure Aaron was still in view. When they finally got to the dock, Kyle stopped at a bench and sat down, letting Aaron stand at the water's edge alone.

Aaron didn't mind Kyle being with him. Kyle never bothered him; he seemed to know the right things to do. In fact, Aaron was just as happy not to be totally alone. He had never just put up with Kyle because he was Matt's little brother; in fact, right now, he liked him in spite of that.

Aaron knew he wouldn't be going over to Matt's place; he wondered if he ever would again. He only wished that he and Nikki had seen Matt as he was, before Nikki had taken her own life; which he now thought had been the wrong decision. And he realized how final that decision had been; and was suddenly unsure of anything he had ever truly believed. And he thought it funny, in a sick sort of way, that Nikki's death and his son, had made him realize this. He stared out at the water; the lights reflected into the ripples that the wind, now getting much stronger, made. He glanced at Kyle and called him over. He wanted him to know that it was okay for him to be there, and he watched as Kyle slouched towards him.

"Come on kiddo, let's go get a beer."

Kyle's face brightened slightly and he walked beside Aaron up the boardwalk

8

Matt walked into his apartment. It was cold and dark. He walked to the window and switched off the air-conditioner, picking up the bucket that caught the drips and dumping it down the sink. He did all this in the dark. Then he switched on the light.

He felt angry and empty, as if a part of him had been stripped away and would never return. He flicked on the T.V., found the baseball game, grabbed a beer from the fridge, and sat in the imitation lazy-boy. He knew how much the others despised him. He was too strong for them; they didn't understand that he had to be that way.

Matt was startled by the knock on the door. He hadn't expected any of them to show up. He let Stacey in and offered her a drink, which she accepted. As he stood at the kitchen counter, the one facing out over the living room, and made her a rye and diet-coke, he watched her move towards the couch. She was simple, he thought, uncomplex, not stupid, just herself. He admired this freedom she had to act and feel the way she wanted to. He handed her the drink and smiled.

"Thanks." She said, smiling back. She drew her legs up onto the couch, tucking her feet under her bum. It was the way she felt most comfortable, and she would do it wherever she felt comfortable, as she always did at Matt's place.

Matt knew Kyle and Aaron wouldn't come over, he didn't need to ask her if they were.

He sat back down, looking towards the television for lack of somewhere better to look. He tried to figure out what was happening in the game, but all the players looked like him, and all the bases looked like mines, and he was afraid to run because everything he touched he destroyed. He took another drink of his beer--a long deep drink--and glanced at Stacey. Not only did she behave simply, she looked simple--plain, he thought. She looked at him; he turned his head away.

"Matt, what is it?"

Leave it to Stacey, Matt thought; the one thing that had always scared him about her was that he always got the feeling that she understood him. Since Nikki had left this feeling had become worse.

Stacey seemed to be paying more attention to him; or maybe, he wondered, he just noticed the attention because Nikki hadn't been around to intercept it. Either way, he wasn't sure he wanted to be understood.

"Nothing," he said.

"You were looking at me."

"If I can look at the queen, I can look at you."

"Nikki used to say that all the time, remember."

She smiled, simply, as if recollecting good thoughts about Nikki, which in fact, was what she was doing, and stared at the television.

Matt watched her. She wasn't beautiful, not like Nikki had been; but, she was far from ugly, too. He was suddenly attracted to her plainness. His eyes roamed her body, which, too, was plain.

Her breasts weren't noticeable unless he looked for them, but they were there, he could see that. In fact, he thought, as he dared to stare a little longer, they were in direct proportion to the rest of her body, which was also small. He pulled his eyes away, as if they had a mind of their own, and had wandered off without him realizing it, and looked back at the baseball game.

Stacey knew his eyes had been turned towards her and she had allowed him to look. She wasn't sure what he was after, but she wanted him to notice her the way she noticed him, so she let him look, without asking questions.

Matt got up for another beer.

Stacey shut the television off.

"What did you do that for. I was watching it."

Stacey laughed, "No you weren't. You were watching me. I wanna talk and so do you."

"No I don't." Matt felt himself getting a little angry, but knew that what Stacey said was true.

"Matt, you don't need to pretend with me. I'm not going to rape you, laugh at what you have inside, and then run out and tell everybody. Come on, let's talk."

Matt sat back down. He took a huge swallow of beer. "You're amazing," he said.

Stacey smiled. She had been right. She hadn't been too sure, when she turned off the baseball game, that she had been right. Now she stared at Matt. He was beautiful, much too good looking for her, but she was his friend and if that was all she would ever be she could adjust.

"Looking at the queen?" Matt smiled.

Stacey blushed, "Almost." She sipped at her drink.

Matt watched her smooth, gentle movements, and realized he had never noticed how graceful she was before. Her red hair looked out of place on top of such elegance, and he wondered if she shouldn't dye it.

Both of them sat there noticing each other; neither one of them said a word.

Matt, unaccustomed to silence, was the first to speak.

"So? What are we talking about?"

Stacey rearranged herself on the couch, letting one foot hang to the floor while she pulled the other one up under her bum. "We're talking about you, and how you feel about everything that's happened. I know you're not as stone-cold as you're letting on. You may as well tell me. I'm staying here until you do."

Matt smiled, "In that case I may never tell you."

Stacey watched him blush slightly, and felt her own face flush. He didn't mean anything by that, she told herself, "Stop joking around, Matt. I'm serious."

"So am I." He spoke softly and into his beer.

Stacey almost got up and left. She hadn't expected him to be like this. What she did was get up and make herself another drink. She stood at the counter and poured it down her throat, then made another one. Now the tables were turned. She was being forced into hiding the way she felt, and Matt was expressing how he felt.

"Stop patronizing me," she said, hoping she was wrong.

Matt came over and stood on the other side of the counter. He stared into her eyes, ran his fingers down the side of her face, and leaned towards her, his lips gently caressing hers. He pulled away, checking the response in her eyes. They were closed. He pressed his lips against hers again, his tongue exploring her mouth. He tasted the rye, and reached farther, wanting to taste everything about her.

Stacey, unaccustomed to this type of attention, allowed Matt the lead. It felt so good, there was no way she was going to stop him. She couldn't fully enjoy the movement of his tongue; she was too tense, too scared, too amazed by what he was doing. Her mind wouldn't let go of the fact that he was too good for her, and she didn't understand how this could be happening.

She wished the thoughts away and for a moment chased his tongue with her own, into his mouth, his beautiful mouth. She pulled back, her tongue, her face, her body, pushing Matt away. He held fast to her arm, and she looked into his eyes.

The greenness of them amazed her; never had she seen green eyes look so beautiful. But there was too much hidden behind them; that's why they were so dark, and she couldn't allow Matt to overcome the feelings he had about Nikki by burying himself in this passion, which Stacey longed to respond to.

She settled her hand gently on his, "Not yet," she said and pulled away.

Aaron and Kyle stood at a small high bar table in 'East End Rafters'. Blue smoke hung between them and circled them.

The bar was fairly empty; it was a Sunday night. Four guys shot pool in the dark corner, and the balls echoed in the small room, while deep laughs and occasional snorts of disgust drifted with the shots.

Kyle looked at the empty grey walls, the un-tiled ceiling, and wondered how Aaron had known about this place.

"I come here to think, sometimes. There's not enough stimuli in this place to distract your thoughts. I like it."

Kyle smiled and butted his cigarette. He was going to have to buy more if he and Aaron stayed out too late. He'd really smoked too much today. This package was supposed to last until noon tomorrow. He had three cigarettes left. He tapped the package against the table. He wasn't quite sure what they were supposed to be thinking about--Nikki, or the kid.

Aaron blew his smoke across the room, away from Kyle. He listened to a pool ball clap its path across the table, and he wondered what it was he was supposed to do now. He swallowed some beer as if that would help him figure it out. He remained confused.

"What do you think I should do?" Aaron asked, his eyes on the game in the corner.

Kyle followed Aaron's gaze, fairly certain the question was his, but not familiar with the role of advisor. He shrugged his shoulders, afraid of the stutter.

Aaron looked at Kyle. The resemblance to Matt was striking. The only noticeable difference being the colour of the eyes, which went unnoticed by most people. They could be twins, Aaron thought--mirror twins, thank God. He smiled, knowing how easily Kyle's sensitivity could be stolen and replaced by his father's and brother's coldness. Aaron would not let that happen. Kyle had chosen to follow him; Aaron wouldn't let him down.

"You're not like your brother."

Kyle blushed and stared at the cigarette pack in his hand. He wanted to light one up, but knew he should be cutting down. He took a swallow of beer and caught Aaron's eyes.

"Thanks." Kyle said, the blush unnoticeable in the dim light.

"Matt hasn't always been like that. I think he started changing when Nikki told him about her and I. It was defensive. He didn't want to get hurt."

Kyle nodded and lit a smoke. He realized it could happen to him, too, if he let it. But he wouldn't let it; he would prepare himself for it, if he could figure out how.

"Maybe that's what happened to your old man, eh? When your mom left him."

Kyle drew hard on the cigarette, realizing he should have tried to answer Aaron's original question and kept the conversation away from himself. "Maybe," he said.

"You don't want to talk about this, do you."

Kyle shook his head, "Not really."

"Okay." Aaron was silent, listening to the laughter in the corner. Another ball clapped its course; chalk scratched the tip of a cue. Aaron took a swig of beer. "So, what am I gonna do. What would you do?" He looked at Kyle.

"I don't know, I guess I'd wanna keep the kid. If he was my own flesh and blood and all. I mean, you may not be perfect, but you've got a lot more going for you than some people out there. You're not gonna beat him or anything." Kyle loved the easy flow of the words. He liked to hear himself speak so well. He went on, caught up in his uncluttered language, "Hell, you don't know what someone else might do to him. At least if he's with you, you know what's happening." He stopped. He felt as if he had said too much; after all, he wasn't used to talking, especially about things he knew nothing about.

"But kids are so...fuck, I don't know." Aaron walked to the bar and grabbed a bar stool, "You want one?"

Kyle joined him. They sat down.

"He's Nikki's." Kyle said, only half realizing the impact this might have on Aaron.

Aaron bent his head down, running his fingers through the long brown hair, and pushing it out of his eyes. He nodded and lit up a cigarette. "I know. I know," he said softly.

"Damn her," Aaron grumbled, "Damn her to hell."

9

Stacey sat facing Matt on the couch, one leg drawn up underneath her. She watched him pout and drink his beer. She touched his hair gently, moving it away from the side of his face, and smiled, her fantasy now real.

"So," Matt said, grinning at her, "what are we talking about?"

Stacey looked deep into his eyes, wanting him, wanting him so bad she almost said forget about the talk. But, she knew, as she'd known for a long time that Matt needed to get rid of some luggage that he'd been carrying around for years. She knew it was the only way their relationship could work, and she didn't want to get sexually involved with him first; she didn't want sex to interfere with their friendship; so, she tied up the passion and searched for her reason, knowing it was the only way to go.

But it was difficult; she hadn't expected him to come on to her the way he had, and she hadn't prepared herself for it.

Matt looked at the digital clock on top of the T.V.. It was 10:35. He wondered how long this was going to take; they both had to work in the morning. He swallowed some of his beer, and listened as Stacey spoke.

"I'm worried about how you're reacting to all of this stuff with Nikki. You seemed to have turned it all off, but I know deep inside you're hurting. Can't you tell me how it makes you feel?"

Matt looked at the beer bottle. He didn't want to tell Stacey, but something inside him made him think it was the right thing to do.

"Come on Matt. It's only me and you. I'm not going to tell anyone. After this you can even go on pretending in front of the others, if you want. It's just me and you who need to know."

"I don't know how I feel," Matt said. "Sometimes I'm angry and sometimes I don't even care. It depends on which way I look at it."

Stacey was silent, waiting for him to continue.

"Sometimes, I feel responsible for what she did, because I wouldn't really let her go, and she knew it. But then, when I don't want to live with that guilt, I tell myself that Aaron was responsible, because he felt so strongly about not having kids, so he forced her into making a decision that she wouldn't have made if it had been my kid."

"You're wrong, Matt." Stacey interrupted, "Nikki would have done this, eventually, whether she had been pregnant or not. In fact, she would've done this no matter what had happened in her life.

It had nothing to do with you, Aaron, Kyle, or me.

It was Nikki that was unhappy, and no matter where she had been or what she had been doing, she would have always been that way. She hated life, Matt, it's as simple as that."

Matt stared at the beer bottle. He couldn't understand how someone could hate life that much. He didn't think there was any excuse in the world for suicide. He had lived through a childhood that had made hell look good, and he still liked life.

"Well, then, she wanted too much out of it," he said.

"Maybe, but she was still the one who had to deal with that, not you or me."

"Okay, so it wasn't my fault. What about Aaron. I think he even knew about all of this. Why didn't he do something? Where does his responsibility lie. If he had really loved her, as everyone seems to think he did, how could he let her do this?"

"That, I'm not sure about. I know I would've done something if I'd known. I don't think he knew about the kid, though. His face went white when Nikki wrote about that. Maybe if he had known about the kid, he would've done something." Stacey stopped; she wasn't certain she was saying the right thing. "That's a question you should ask Aaron, if you want to know the true answer. Only he knows."

Matt stared at the empty beer bottle. Maybe he would ask Aaron; he didn't know for sure. He knew he and Nikki hadn't been right for each other; it had just been something they got trapped into and used to; it hadn't been real. So, he wasn't angry with Aaron for taking Nikki away. In fact, he should be grateful to Aaron for rescuing both of them. But, he did still care about Nikki, and he needed to know why Aaron hadn't told anyone that Nikki felt this way.

"Maybe I will," he said, "if I ever see him again."

"Why do you say that?"

"The way I spoke to him tonight. All the sex stuff. You don't think he's going to come back for more of that, do you?"

Stacey chuckled. "He knew you were angry, and maybe...jealous?" She looked at Matt carefully.

He nodded his head, "Yeah, I was jealous. But they were right. Nikki and I weren't meant for each other. I guess I've known that for a while. It's just hard to admit after so many years together."

Stacey smiled. That's what she had needed to hear. Now there was only one more thing that she needed to hear.

They sat in silence for several minutes. Matt got up for another beer. Stacey declined another drink; she didn't want to be hung-over and tired at work tomorrow.

"Have I said enough?" Matt asked, a smile playing on his lips, as he sat back down with his beer.

"There's one more thing that worries me about you." Stacey needed to choose her words carefully. "Nikki brought it up in her note, right near the beginning."

Matt thought about it. He couldn't think of what it might be, "What?" he asked.

"Your father." Stacey said, searching Matt's face for clues about how he would respond to this. She watched him take a large swallow of beer and set the bottle on the coffee table in front of him.

"What about him."

"Did he beat you, the way he beat Kyle?"

"What has that got to do with any of this?"

"It has to do with you."

Matt stood up, grabbing his beer, and paced the living room; he stopped at the window, looking out.

"Come on Matt, admit it, and we'll go from there."

"Okay, God damn it, he beat me, too. What's the fucking point? It's not something I try to think about, okay. I like to forget about it."

"Pretend it didn't happen?"

"Sometimes...yeah. I hate the son-of-a-bitch."

"Yet tonight," and Stacey squirmed as she trod on this ground, "you treated Kyle just like he does, and, at times, reacted just like he would have. Do you realize that?"

Matt glared at his reflection in the window. He hated his old man and now he was becoming him and, suddenly, he hated himself. "But how can I stop it?" He asked quietly.

Stacey walked over to him. She put her arms around his waist and looked into his eyes. "Admitting it is a start," and she raised herself with her toes until her lips met his. She pressed herself against him, feeling his body respond to hers.

Matt set the beer bottle on the window ledge and pulled Stacey closer. They drew their lips away from each other, exploring eyes. Matt hugged her, feeling himself rise.

Stacey, pressed against Matt's body, could feel the bulge in his pants. She rubbed against him. Never before had she wanted someone so badly. She found his lips, again, explored his mouth with her tongue, allowing him to do the same. Then she felt him pick her up. She wrapped her legs around his waist, stared into his eyes, found his lips again, and allowed him to carry her to the bedroom. She caressed herself against his body as they moved.

Matt gently stood her up in the bedroom. He undid the buttons on her blouse, his fingers shaking slightly. It had never been like this with Nikki. He felt as if he was going to explode with passion.

Sweat beaded on his forehead already. He removed Stacey's top, and fumbled with her bra. She helped him, gracefully, smiling, he stared at her nakedness and pulled off his t-shirt.

Stacey felt his cold fingers on her breasts. She stared at his chest, wanting more. She reached down, unbuttoning his jeans, unzipping them. She ran her hands down his back, down his pants, pulling them down, feeling his perfect cheeks, she slid the pants down to his ankles. He kicked his feet, stepping out of his pants. Stacey slid his underwear off and stared longingly at his manness, and then into his eyes, as Matt's hands removed her jeans and panties, caressing her buttocks. She felt the chills of longing build up and her nipples hardened in response to his tongue, as both bodies gently laid upon the bed.

10

It was late. Aaron and Kyle were still in the bar, listening to the rain, now, which had started soon after the pool-balls had stopped. They were both on the afternoon shift the next day; the present hour didn't bother them. They had each had five beers; Kyle was out of cigarettes and bumming from Aaron, who didn't mind.

Aaron wondered how life could get so confusing all of a sudden. Everything he had believed in was now ripped apart. And he realized how wrong he might have been, about everything--kids, Nikki, life. He ordered another beer.

Kyle, not a heavy drinker, wasn't sure if he should have another one or not. He still had to go home and, considering the time, his old man was certain to be there. "Can I stay at your place tonight?" he asked.

"Sure. Having another?"

"Yeah, why not."

"After this one we'll go to my place and sit and not talk, okay?"

Kyle laughed, "The beer's cheaper there."

"Don't have any. We'll have to get into the rye."

Kyle laughed, certain that Aaron was just joking. He knew Aaron hardly ever got drunk; he had this thing about always being in control of himself. Kyle had seen him let loose a couple of times, but not often.

"So," Kyle asked, "what're you going to do about the kid?"

Aaron shrugged his shoulders and shook his head.

"I had a friend, once, in grade school," Kyle said, "who was adopted. He was only eight years old, and his dad beat the shit out of him so bad, that he never made it back to the third grade.

It used to scare me to death when my dad hit me that the same thing was gonna happen. I was lucky. All I got were a few broken bones, bumps, and bruises. This kid got a life sentence in a home for retarded kids. You don't know what kind of parents are gonna adopt him."

"Nikki said she took care of it. I trust her." But being so uncertain about everything else right now, Aaron didn't know if he believed this or not. He wanted Nikki back. He wanted the kid too. But, he didn't know if he wanted the kid without Nikki.

"I'm only twenty-six years old. What the hell am I gonna do with a kid on my own."

"You'd be great. If I was that little kid, I'd want you for a father."

Aaron smiled, "Thanks Kyle. But think about it. I don't know anything about kids."

"You were a kid, once. Can't you remember what that was like."

"No. I hated being a kid. The world's too big for adults. How the hell's a kid supposed to get to know it."

"You'll teach him."

Aaron laughed. "Look Kyle, almost everything I ever believed in has been flushed down the toilet by Nikki. I don't have anything to teach anyone. I don't know anything."

Kyle was silent. He hadn't realized Aaron's whole philosophy on life, which Kyle had admired, had been destroyed. He didn't know what to say. He stayed quiet.

They finished their beers and walked to Aaron's place in the rain. They were soaked when they got there. Aaron gave Kyle a track-suit and poured himself a rye, straight-up. He gulped it back and made another one. His hair dripped onto the counter, his wet clothes clinging to his slight frame.

Kyle, having been in the bathroom, changing, looked at Aaron with a bottle in one hand and a half-empty glass in the other, dripping on the kitchen floor, and staring into space. He watched Aaron dump the drink down his throat, with only a slight look of distaste on his face as he set the glass down and filled it up again.

"Here," Kyle said, holding out the towel Aaron had given him. "Dry yourself off before you catch pneumonia."

"I hope I catch pneumonia and die." Aaron took the towel, flipping it over his shoulder, and his drink and went into the bedroom. "Make yerself a drink, if ya want," he yelled just before he shut the door.

Kyle went to the fridge and grabbed a coke. He figured at least one of them should stay sober, although he was feeling a little light-headed from the beers he had drank. He didn't much like rye, anyway. He cracked open the pop, took a long swallow, and sat down on the couch.

Aaron came out, filled his glass, and plopped into the large pillow on the floor in front of the couch. He flipped on the T.V.. "Whadda ya wanna watch?"

"Not much on at one o'clock in the morning."

"That what time it is? You can have the spare bedroom whenever you wanna go to bed, kay?"

"Sure. Thanks." Kyle was tired, but thought he would stay up a little longer, just to see if Aaron was going to be alright.

Aaron flipped the channels. He couldn't concentrate on the pictures that kept moving and flipping back. He burped and laughed, swaying slightly on the pillow, almost spilling his drink, which he then drank.

Kyle saw Aaron's head fall back on the couch and his eyes close. He watched him be still for several minutes, before turning off the T.V. and going to bed.

Aaron woke up with a start, kinking his neck; he held it still for several seconds, afraid to move it again. He pulled himself up from the sprawled position he had been in and sighed. His head throbbed and his mouth was dry; he sat starring at the dead television set.

The sight he had just seen in his dream had left him in a cold sweat and he took off the t-shirt he had on, and was just about to remove the track pants, when he remembered he had company. He looked around him. The place was dark except for the glow coming out of the bathroom. Aaron wondered which one of them Kyle had left the light on for. He pulled himself up onto the couch and wiped the sweat from his forehead with the t-shirt.

The little kid in his dream had been him, but not exactly him. Sometimes his hair had seemed to change colour, as if he were blonde instead of dark. Aaron tried to remember what the man in the dream had looked like, but he couldn't.

It hadn't been anyone he knew; he wondered if it was someone he had maybe met once or twice. In the dream he had seemed familiar; now, Aaron could only remember that he had been large, extremely large, at least six feet, five inches, with a beer belly that hung out over his pants. He also remembered that he or the kid, anyway, had been scared to death of him. Then he remembered the bat the guy had been swinging around and realized why the kid had been frightened.

"Shit," he said, and went to the fridge for a glass of milk. He pulled some aspirin down from the cupboard, shook three into his hand, and swallowed them with the milk. He lit up a cigarette and went back to the couch.

He knew what his subconscious was trying to say to him through the dream, but he didn't want to listen to it. He flicked on the T.V..

He looked at the clock and knew there wouldn't be anything but old movies on at this hour in the morning. When the screen finally came into view, a blonde kid, who looked about nine or ten, was being chased by an older kid with a stick, around a room filled with coffins. Aaron, having seen the movie before, realized it was 'Oliver Twist' and switched the channel before picking up the 'T.V. Guide' to see what else might be on.

He turned the channel to watch 'VJ: Steve Anthony', hoping that, at least, it would be safe. After his dream and the scene from 'Oliver', he didn't think he needed any more subtle lessons from his subconscious; at this moment he was certain he would go and get his son, rescuing him from the tyrant who was sure to be his father if Aaron didn't step in. When the video 'The Living Years' came on, Aaron watched the singer with his son on the screen, and realized that he really did want to see the child that was his. He turned the T.V. off and went to bed.

EPILOGUE

Aaron walked slowly towards the grave, Troy's legs wrapped around his hip, an arm around his neck, thumb in his mouth, "Dere, daddy?"

Aaron smiled and hoisted the child farther up his hip, "Almost, sweetie. Just up there. See where those flowers are?"

Aaron's face turned serious as he neared the site.

"Down daddy."

Aaron set the child down, his eyes fastened to the flowers, then to the stone, and finally down the full length of where she would be laying. He turned suddenly, remembering Troy, and saw him circling a tree as if he were a plane. Aaron looked back at the grave.

"At least you left me something." He paused and pointed towards Troy, "He's beautiful. Just like you. Dark brown wavy hair and beautiful blue eyes." Aaron knelt down and picked up a flower, holding it to his nose. "I know I've told you that before," he said quietly, "it's just, well, he means so much to me." Aaron paused, setting down the flowers.

"I've got some shitty news Nikki. Kyle died last week. Got caught in some fog on a two-lane highway and some drunk crossed the centre line. Killed instantly, thank God. Hey, maybe you'll see him sometime. So this was all useless. Kyle's gone, and Stacey and Matt are getting married. You wouldn't have hurt anymore people." Aaron glanced towards Troy, watching him fly around the tree– arms spread as if they were wings. He looked back at the stone and then down as he pulled grass up with his hands.

"What am I supposed to tell him Nikki, that his mother thought she'd be happier without us? Well, I do hope you're happy. There isn't anything in the world I wish more than that. Or, do I tell him you figured we'd be happier without you? He'll want to know why." He looked back towards Troy, "The only thing I'm angry about is that I have to tell him. Guess I'll just read him your note, eh?...yeah, I guess that's what I'll have to do." He stood up, brushing the seat of his pants. "See ya later, Nikki. I still love you."

He walked towards the tree.

"Daddy, pwane."

"Yeah, I see. Let daddy help," and Aaron lifted the two-year-old child into the air and flew him back to the car.

THE END

J. E Badham

Born in England, moved to Canada at the age of three.
Started writing early in life and has a novel to publish in
the near future as well as a chap book of poetry. Lives in a
small village in southern Ontario, where she taught
elementary school for ten years. Has a special interest in
mental health issues and all the people it touches.

DANK HOUSE MANOR PUBLISHING

Other titles

iDrip – The Play - Neil S. Reddy

Interzone Xpress Boogie - Neil S. Reddy

The Wanting Wolf - Iris Barnes Lawrence